TABLE OF CONTENTS

FORWARD

My novel started out with a different idea. The California Legislature, in legislation signed by Governor Jerry Brown on October 22, 2015, had banned the use of Redskins as a mascot at any of the state's high schools. I found this very upsetting. I dealt with my anger by writing a blog post and letter to my local newspaper accusing those who voted in favor of this (including both my state senator and my state assemblyman) of doing the equivalent of "murdering" an elderly man.

Chowchilla High School was 99 years old when this happened. If my grandfather were still alive, he too would have been 99. I wrote the book with the premise Reddy Redskin was born the year the high school opened, an infant Native American who had been treasured throughout the life of the high school, and who in all likelihood, would have gone to Chowchilla Union High School with Grandfather if Reddy had been real. This is, in fact, the year Reddy was considered to be born. A memorial erected by E Clampus Vitus in front of the school office memorializes him as having lived from 1916 to 2016. This recognizes the high school was able to use the Redskins as its mascot until the winter sports season of 2016-2017.

When I published the first edition of this book, I had been told the school did not start using the Redskins as a sports mascot until 1928. If that were true, Reddy Redskin would have only been 88 when he died. He would have been the same age as my mother-in-law, who, as I write this, is still very much with us. Whether Reddy Redskin was 99, 100 or only 88 when he died, had he been real, one could certainly understand the outrage over the murder of a beloved elderly man. But he was real, even though not in a human sense.

If the legislature had truly understood California history, they would have known that even in 1916, Californians didn't like what had been done to the Native Americans in the 19th century. In early 20th century Chowchilla, around 1912, the people of that day chose the community's name to honor the Chaushilha tribe. I can understand Redskin was used long before that as a derogatory term by people who didn't appreciate the humanity of those with darker skin than theirs. But in the early 20th century, it was selected as my high school's mascot by people who wanted to honor the Native Americans.

They misspelled Chaushilha too, way back when. How ignorant. Sort of like naming the mascot for a term that wasn't what the tribe called themselves. Shall we stop calling our city "Chowchilla" because of that? Shall we order the current day tribe, which has also adopted the name "Chowchilla" to change its spelling back to the correct way of the ancient tribe? I think not. The city, the school, and even the tribe have a history now as Chowchilla. Changing it to Chaushilha would be silly. I also think the Legislature erred when it ordered the school to go against its 99-year history and change its mascot.

My original book would have expanded the "murder" of Reddy Redskin to a fictional story about a man who lived for nearly a century in Chowchilla, and who would have been touched by the events of that century. But to understand his history, it was necessary to look back into what his great-grandparents experienced after the discovery of gold in California in 1849. In my research into what that might have been, I learned it was much more than White men coming into California and telling every Native American they met the land they were standing on no longer belonged to them. It was, for the most part, much worse than that. In fact, for Reddy Redskin's family to have even survived as a traditional Native American family, in Chowchilla, all the way to 1928, they would have had to have had things go fairly well for them compared to what most Native Americans experienced.

In my research, I decided to document how a Native American boy, born in the very real village of Shehamniu in 1840 would have been affected. He would remember 1848, when his village still lived the way it always had even though its population had already decreased due to early 19th century explorers and Catholic padres bringing deadly diseases to California. He would have noticed changes to the food supply, lost loved ones to these diseases and lost more loved ones in a war between Whites and Native Americans. Lastly, he would and be forced into slavery like so many children of his time. Thankfully for Reddy Redskin, this forefather of his was taken in by a relatively kind master.

The master wouldn't have had much reason to be in mid-19th century Chowchilla unless he was growing wheat or other grains. Nothing much else grew there before farmers started diverting water out of the rivers (Chowchillla and San Joaquin) around 1910. There was no "city" even to speak of until 1912 when O. A. Robertson created one out of some of the 108,000 acres of western prairie he himself had just purchased from the federal land office. There was nothing but fertile soil, and next to the rivers, enough groundwater to grow wheat without irrigation. So, this early day settler grew wheat.

The master's family would have had even less reason to be in Chowchilla. But how would a single man keep from going crazy with no one to keep him company? He had to bring his family with him. That means, he and his wife and his children had no one but the nearby Native Americans to relate to. And, if he had a daughter close to the same age as the Native American boy, that meant the desire for romance most teen-agers have experienced in some way, could only have been experienced by her with a Native American boy. That love would have been stronger than a teen-age crush of today, as there was no one else they could have felt that way about. If you grew up like a brother or sister to your friend, that friendship could easily turn into a powerful love.

Whether White or Native American, these children would have seen some of the cities near them grow considerably larger. Not so much the ones in the San Joaquin Valley. They didn't get started until at least the late 19th Century. But San Francisco, Sacramento, Benicia and a few other cities incorporated in 1850, the same year California was admitted to the Union. Sonora had incorporated prior to July 4, 1851 when all of California celebrated its first Independence Day as part of the United States. Mariposa and what is now known as Oakhurst have never incorporated, but they too swelled in population in the last half of the 19th century.

This certainly would have had many ramifications, even for those who did not live in those cities. The Californians, wherever they lived, would have been affected by becoming part of the United States, and all that other parts of the country went through in the mid-19th century as well. This would include the continued push for westward expansion, the increased reliance on machinery, and certainly, the Civil War.

With all these ramifications, I realized the story of the mid-19th century's impact on Chowchilla, even though it wasn't really around then, still needed to be told. Instead of a brief look at the 19th century before delving into Reddy Redskin's life and life story, we all need to understand how the 19th century impacted our story. Thus, my book is the story of the first "Chowchillans," that is, the last surviving members of the ancient Chaushilha tribe in Shehamniu. There were other villages besides Shehamniu, including those in the mountains. The membership of the current-day Chowchilla tribe draws from the descendants of all those villages. But for Shehamniu residents alone, the years of 1849 to 1865 were rich in history, and that is what this book attempts to portray.

I do offer some disclaimers: Most of the events and places, including Shehamniu and the Young Women's Seminary were very real during the years 1849-1865, although it is debatable whether Shehamniu wasn't completely wiped out by 1851. Also real were many people mentioned in this story, other than the residents of Shehamniu and the Eastman family. Those real include the Native American chiefs from the Chauchila and Ahwahneechee tribes, and the White settlers who held positions of power in Sonora, Mariposa and Oakhurst at that time. The two state governors and two of the three staff members named at Young Women's Seminary also were real, as was the pastor of the Episcopal Church in Stockton and the young Native American boy who attended in its early days. However, there was to my knowledge, no Eastman family, or if there was, it is no relation to the Eastmans who inhabited Chowchilla later. There also, to my knowledge were no residents of Shehamniu named Wabakashiek, Tashi, Macha, Aloette, Dyami or any of the other Native American names I gave my characters.

Also, the Chaushilha and Ahwahneechee tribes were very real. In my story, the Chauchilha and Chaushilha tribes are separate entities, and I have seen research indicating there may have actually been two distinct tribes, one Yokut, one Miwok, that spelled and pronounced their names the same way. Additional research indicates, by 1849, these two tribes were completely intermingled through marriages. However, other than in my story, there was no division between the Chaushilha and Chauchila tribes.

The entire Chaushilha tribe, as well as any others in the San Joaquin Valley, were generally thought to be sub-tribes of the Yokut tribe. However, the Yokut tribes were arranged by divisions. "North Valley Yokuts" occupied the area where Shehamniu was and Chowchilla is. "Foothill Yokuts" may have occupied the area where Oakhurst is, including where Okhumhurst once was. To the north of Oakhurst, modern maps of Native American tribal lands show a division between Yokut and Miwok tribal lands. This division appears to be along the Chowchilla River, which would place the modern-day Mariposa in Miwok territory, but its near neighbor, Ahwahnee, in Yokut territory. Yosemite National Park, north of Oakhurst and east of Ahwahnee, showcases its Miwok history far more than any Yokut history it may also have. I therefore made an imaginary plateau along the Chowchilla River a dividing line between the Chaushilha, Chauchila and Ahwahneechee tribes.

INTRODUCTION
As might have been told by
William "Wabakashiek" Redskin

Imagine your entire culture being taken away from you. You wouldn't like it, would you? Yet that's exactly what happened to me, many, many years ago. It all started when I was a boy. First they started encroaching on our hunting grounds, which meant we had less to eat unless we bought meat in their stores. Then they kidnapped some of us, and tried to make us live like White people. Then they started growing wheat and corn and later, cotton and many other crops on what had been OUR land.

My name is William Redskin. I was born on March 4, 1840 in a village called Shehamniu. Back then, my people called me Wabakahshiek, which means "The Red Cloud."
Shehamniu is not too far from a place you may know as Chowchilla. If you don't know Chowchilla, it's a town that by the 21st century has reached a population of approximately 15,000 people – 20,000 if you count those who live on the vast acres of farms surrounding the city. It's still a small town as far as California cities of the 21st century go. But it's huge compared with what Shehamniu was, and even to what Chowchilla became in my time.

Everything is different from when I was born. Heck, things started changing a lot before I was even 10. If it weren't for the fact that Chowchilla is named for my tribe, the Chaushilha, and the high school's mascot was the same name a White man bestowed on me when I was 11, I even wonder if kids today going to that high school would even know Native Americans ever lived in this area.

In some ways, even by the time I died in the early 20th century, life was easier. For instance, I was really glad I never had to grind acorns into acorn meal with grinding rocks after I was 11 years old. Using pre-ground wheat flour was much better. I am also really glad I started living in a house when I was 25 years old. I liked that better than living in a wiki-up. That's how I lived until then. A wiki-up, or hut, is just a bunch of sticks tied tightly together and topped with grass, and whomever lives there sleeps on bear skins. If they're lucky. For some of my years, I slept on the cold hard ground.

I spent most of my life, after the age of 11, working on a farm. Most of the time, we just grew wheat. We planted wheat seeds. We watched them grow. We hoed weeds that were choking the wheat. We harvested the wheat. We hauled the wheat to ranchers and merchants who would pay us for the wheat. Wheat, wheat, wheat. When I was 18 years old, we started growing barley and oats for a big cattle rancher. Much later, we finally figured out how to grow things other than grain!

Still, it wasn't as much fun as when I was a young boy. Back then, women and children hunted for seeds. Men hunted for animals. If we didn't hunt, we didn't eat. And when we got done hunting, cooking and eating, we had time to do a lot of fun things that were very important to our culture. We played games like Spear and Hoops. We told stories like the story of the Eagle and the Crow. And we spent a great deal of time just appreciating the birds, the trees, the sun and the stars.

Things really changed a lot when I was 11. That's when the man who would become my father-in-law kidnapped me and made me his slave. Oh wait, you thought California was a free state? Maybe if you were Black, although I don't remember ever meeting any Black people in my lifetime. It definitely wasn't free if you were Native American.

My master was kinder than some. And, he had Eliza, the most beautiful girl in all of Shehamniu, even if she was White. Eliza eventually became my wife. We had a bunch of little Redskins, although almost all of them eventually changed their name, both the girls and the boys.

My father-in-law, Ralph Eastman, had some dumb ideas at first. He thought he could raise me better than my own Pa could. Or maybe he just wanted me and my friends' help on the farm, and the only way it was going to happen was if he kidnapped us. It's not that we didn't want to help him. We just kind of got caught in the middle of a battle between Red and White, between the old way of life our ancestors represented, and the new way of life he represented. Eastman and the other White men never really gave much thought to what we wanted. At least not at first. They didn't even see us as fully human.

I will give Eastman credit. He always was nice to me and the other two boys he kidnapped. Although he never trusted my friends, he did eventually come to trust me. When he got to know the others in my village, he treated them with respect. And when Eliza came back from college espousing the truth that all human beings are created equally – and that I personally was the finest example of this she had ever seen - he genuinely accepted me as part of the family.

That's a whole lot more than most White men and women did. Honestly, I don't know how I could have lived within 10 miles of some of those jerks. And yet, some of those I knew as a boy had no choice. The White men came, took their land and forced them to do as they were told. Some of them raped our women, some of them killed our men for no reason. And all of them felt they were so much better than us. They weren't.

When I was an old man, White people had come to realize they had made some big mistakes. They tried their best to make it right. In 1912, they named a town after my people. Four years later, they built a high school in that town, and in 1928, after I and everyone else from my village was dead and gone, they named the mascot Redskins. That's the name the Whites had always called my people. I'm pretty sure by then they meant no disrespect. It was just what they had always done.

But, by 1928, their ways had taken over. Our ways were gone. The good thing is people try to remember their history. And our history. If they didn't, they probably would do the same stupid things people did in my day. Like trample on other people's rights, just because they think themselves smarter or better than those other people.

CHAPTER 1

In 1840, when Wabakashiek was born, his family lived in the village of Shehamniu on the floor of a great valley that would later become known as the San Joaquin Valley. Although Shehamniu was the primary city of a tribe known as the Chaushilha, fewer than 100 people (most of them related somehow to Wabakashiek) lived in this village. The tribe had never been large, perhaps because in ancient days it had split from a larger tribe, the Chauchila, who settled in the foothills above the great valley.

By the time Wabakashiek was born, it was smaller than it had been historically. In the early 19th century, before Wabakashiek's time, the men of the village had traded with the Costanoan tribe. This tribe, as well as some of the Yokuts who lived farther west than Shehamniu, were exposed to tuberculosis and other diseases by White explorers and even Catholic padres. Thus, when the men of Shehamniu traded with these villages, they unknowingly brought the disease back to their women and children. The Native Americans had no immunity to tuberculosis in the early 19th century, so Shehamniu was decimated by a wave of epidemics. One last tuberculosis outbreak, when Wabakashiek was 3 years old, took 75 percent of the remaining villagers, including his own mother.

As was the case in any Native American Yokut village, there were no stores, post offices, churches or schools in Shehamniu. There were simply dozens of mostly small, single-room homes forming a circle. The people of Shehamniu made these homes, known as wiki-ups, by bending tall, slender branches over their heads into dwellings large enough to accommodate a family. They then covered these homes with thatch made from the native grasses growing on their land.

Some wiki-ups were only the size of modern-day tents. This was fine for Wabakashiek and his father Tashi, who lived by themselves after the deadly tuberculosis epidemic of 1843. Some families needed larger homes. For instance, Wabakashiek had an increasingly larger number of cousins, so his Uncle Achachak and Aunt Macha added onto their wiki-up every few years to accommodate their growing family. In Shehamniu, the families within the village gathered around campfires built nightly in the middle of the circle. Here they danced as they had for generations, played games and listened to the tribal elders tell stories. These stories conveyed truths of nature, and helped children to understand the Yokut ways.

When Wabakashiek was 9 years old, his father, Tashi and his grandfather, Chief Red Hawk, began taking him on hunting trips. Before then, they didn't have to go very far. In those days, many deer frequently wandered from the mountain areas just above their village to graze on the grass in the lowlands. Some days, they would wander right into the village. There were also quail, doves, pigeons, coyotes, foxes and rabbits close by. In the higher elevations, elks and antelopes roamed. Sometimes they too would roam down closer to the village. The men also placed traps on the river, where they captured trout, perch and other fish.

In the late 1840s, the animal supply had started mysteriously dwindling. One day, Tashi, Wabakashiek and the other men and older boys from the village paddled up the river all the way to the two plateaus. Although they didn't keep track of time this way, the White settlers who had arrived in the area north of here knew the day as November 2, 1849.

It was hard work rafting up river. Most of the rafts had four men sitting on them, each paddling to overcome the push of the downhill stream. Wabakashiek and some of the other boys weren't strong enough to be much help with that, so their rafts had four men and the weight of boys weighing up to 100 lbs. Still, the supply of animals was usually better at the higher elevations than downstream. As they arrived at where the river split two plateaus, they were disappointed to have not seen any animals. The plateaus were supposed to be the end of the line.

Above the plateaus, to the east, was the boundary the Chaushilhas shared with their neighboring tribes, the Chauchila and the Ahwaneechee. Decades before, the elders of the Chaushilha, Chauchila and Ahwaneechee tribes had smoked peace offerings, agreeing to keep their villages and hunting grounds separate. The Chaushilhas were to remain downstream from the plateaus. Upstream, the Chauchila had the north side of the river and the Ahwaneechee were to remain on the south side of the river.

As they looked up the river, over on the Chauchila side, something caught their eye. In a field of grass, they saw three strange looking animals. They were larger than deer, and redder in color. Although most of their bodies were covered with short reddish-brown hair, long black hair flowed down their necks.

There were about 40 men and boys in the rafts. Most of the rafts carried three men, but some also carried less than full-grown boys like Wabakashiek. As they had paddled up to the plateau from their village, they had engaged in lively conversation back and forth. But when they saw these strange animals, they fell silent. Quietly, they paddled up to the field where the horses were grazing.

To their surprise, the strange animals did not try to run from them. It became obvious they could take the horses alive. But how would they fit them into the rafts? Tashi wasn't going to wait to find out. He took an arrow out of his quiver, and started to fit the feathered end into his bow string.

"Don't shoot yet," Chief Red Hawk cried out in Yokutsan, the language all three tribes spoke in that region.
Tashi questioned his chief's logic. If they were seen or heard by Chauchila they would lose their opportunity to kill these beautiful animals. They would have to return home to the women and children, and tell them acorn bread and mush would be all they could eat for a while. But, disobeying the chief might mean he would end up with the arrow through his heart. Without a word, he put the arrow back into his quiver.

"Achachak, Kajika and Wachinksapa, out of the boats," Chief Red Hawk yelled. "You are the mightiest warriors! Grab the necks of these animals, and see if you can jump on them!"
The horses noticed the commotion, and their ears perked when three of the men got out of the rafts and headed towards them. But they didn't try to run. To the men's surprise, the horses let them get on top of them. Each man slapped his horse in the direction of downstream. The horses turned, and ran exactly where their riders wanted them to go.

Chief Red Hawk ordered the rest of the men to turn their rafts around. Even though they were paddling downstream, the horses made the trip back to Shehamniu much faster than the rafts did. The three men riding them hung on for dear life. The rest of the hunting party wondered if they would ever see Achachak, Kajika and Wahchinksapa again.

"Papa, why did Chief Red Hawk order Achachak, Kajika and Wachinksapa out of the boats and onto those big animals?" Wabakashiek asked.

"I don't know," Tashi answered. "But since we no longer have Achachak to help us, I'm going to need you to paddle. It's downstream. It will be easier. Can you do this for me?"

"Sure Papa," Wabakashiek said. "I'm really strong."
As they paddled down the stream, something else caught Wabakashiek's eye.

"Look Papa," he whispered "A deer!"

Wabakashiek had been hunting in the village for several years, and had killed quite a few frogs and squirrels. He had even killed a few jackrabbits. That was just play though. This time, he had a chance to feed his entire family. He loaded his own bow with an arrow, pointed it in the direction of the deer and pulled back on the bow string. Within seconds, the arrow hit the deer in the side. Since none of the grown men or older boys were helping him, Wabakashiek sailed another arrow in his direction, then another. Struck three times, the deer collapsed to the ground.

"Great job, Wabakashiek!" cried out Chief Red Hawk from his raft, as the rest of the hunting party clapped and hollered "Wabakshiek! Way to go! You will feed many people venison tonight!"

The entire hunting party paddled over to the riverbank where the deer lie. Tashi ran up the hill, grabbed the deer, and put it into his raft, right where Achachak had been sitting on the uphill journey. Somehow, even though the deer weighed more than Achachak, it seemed lighter in the raft than when just two men and one 65-pound boy were there. As they paddled downstream, Wabakashiek noticed a red hawk flying above them, as if it was leading them back to Shehamniu. Since the hawk was the spirit animal for him, his father, and his grandfather, they revered these birds and never shot them.

When Achachak, Kajika and Wachinksapa returned riding the strange animals, with none of the rest of the hunting party with them, the women were curious and somewhat afraid. When Macha, wife of Achachak, saw the three men on the strange animals, she ran out to them.

"What has happened to Tashi and Wabakashiek and the others?" she cried out. Tashi and Wabakashiek lived next to them in the village, and she had cared for her nephew Wabakashiek the last six years. That was when her sister, Kaliska, died from tuberculosis.

"Look at these beautiful animals," Achachak said. "They could feed many villagers. But they also run faster than rafts float down river! Maybe we should keep them to get where we need to go."

A few minutes later, the rafts with the rest of the hunting party returned to Shehamniu. The village began rejoicing. The hunting party had safely returned, and Tashi was carrying a deer!

"We're all going to eat well tonight, except for Wabakashiek," Tashi said. Hearing that, Macha smiled even more. That meant her young nephew had killed the deer. Chaushilha tradition required that boys not eat the first game animal they killed. This taught the boys the importance of sharing their hunted prey with others in the village.

Wabakashiek had forgotten that rule, and was disappointed to be reminded he would not be eating deer meat that night. He crossed his arms onto his chest and looked down, trying not to cry. At his age, if he cried, his father or even another man might lash him with the cat-tails that grew in a marshland next to the river. Cat tails were sharp, and could cut through a boy's skin. The Chaushilha tribe punished their boys for crying in this way because they were fiercer warriors than the other nearby tribes, and wanted the young boys to be physically, emotionally and mentally strong.

 Macha put her arm around Wabakashiek, led him to the flat rock where they ate their meals, and handed him a wedge of freshly-baked acorn bread. On top of the wedge, she placed a fistful of acorn mush. She also handed Wabakashiek a bunch of blackberries. These grew wild on the bank of the river, but Macha and other women in the village carefully maintained the vines to yield as many blackberries as possible.

This made Wabakashiek feel a little better, because his Aunt Macha was the best acorn bread baker in all of Shehamniu. Her acorn mush also was tasty. Not quite as tasty as deer meat, but then, if he hadn't seen the deer, everyone in the village would have been eating acorn mush with bread that night.

While men and boys at least Wabakashiek's age hunted, the women and younger children would hike up to the oak tree grove, a mile away. If the children were too young to walk, their mothers carried them on their backs in basket-like cradles. For as long as he could remember, Wabakashiek had helped Macha gather acorns, putting them into baskets she wove from the tule reeds that grew in the river near the village. Just a month earlier, before the temperatures were cold, they had taken two baskets. Macha had carried back one basket full on her head, while Wabakashiek and one of his cousins carried the other, walking lockstep back down the trail to their village.

The women and children then spread the acorns out to dry. After a few days of drying, he would help Macha and her children crack the acorns open. They did this by pounding the acorns with rocks until the hard shell surrounding the acorns crunched. They could then break pieces of shell away, revealing a much softer acorn center.

Macha, and every other woman in the village, had a rock shaped like a bowl, and another as long as a man's longest finger, and as wide as three fingers. They would put the acorn flesh into the bowl-shaped rock, then use the smaller rock to grind it into a meal that looked something like modern-day bread crumbs. Although Macha started the process, she expected Wabakashiek and all of her children to take turns grinding the acorn flesh as well. Getting it down to the right texture could take a long time, but it made the bread and mushes taste so much better.

After the women and children ground the acorns into meal, the women took sharper rocks and dug holes deep into the ground. They would then line the holes with grape leaves, spread the meal out over the leaves and pour boiling water over the meal several times. This important step removed the bitter taste of the acorns, and allowed the meal to form into an acorn cake.

The women easily lifted these cakes from the hole, mixed cooled water into the cake, and formed a soft dough. From this dough, they made acorn bread. On the nights before they wanted to bake bread, Chaushilha women placed large flat rocks into the village campfires. In the morning, when the campfire was nothing but embers, these rocks were warm enough to turn dough spread over them into a soft bread. Chaushilha women also could make mush with the acorn meal. They would place the meal into tightly woven baskets, add water and place small fire-heated rocks into the baskets. They had to stir the mush quickly, otherwise the hot rocks would burn holes into their baskets.

"That was very good Aunt Macha," Wabakashiek said after finishing his bread, mush and grapes. Do you want me to help you cook my deer now?"

"No, you cannot even touch the deer, Wabaskashiek," she replied. "Go help your father and your uncle make some more arrows. You obviously need some more, and so will Achachak if he's going to kill those animals he, Kajika and Wachinksapa brought back. Looks like you'll be able to have some good meat tomorrow night!"

But while Wabakashiek ate his meal, and Macha began preparation of the deer, Chief Red Hawk addressed his fellow hunters and the other men of the village about the animals Achachak, Kajika and Wachinksapa had returned with.

"We should not kill these animals," Chief Red Hawk said. "Our village's other hunting party was more successful, and they killed enough deer to last us several weeks. We will keep these animals. They will help us when we go to meet with the other tribes."

Shehamniu was nearly in the corner of three historical divisions of Native American tribal lands. The Chaushilha were was part of the "Northern Valley Yokuts" division, residing just west of the "Foothill Yokuts" division that included the Ahwaneechee and its communities of Ahwahnee and Okumhurst. The Chauchila, although similar in name to their neighbors, were not a sub-tribe of the Yokuts. They instead were a subtribe of the Miwoks.

Ahwahnee has maintained its name into the 21st century, although it has long since ceased to be a Native American village. Okhumhust is a portion of the area now known as Oakhurst, but for a time in the late 19th century was known as Fresno Flats. The Chauchila lived in a village called Mariposa. In the 21st century, a modern-day Mariposa encompasses both the Native American village area, and a nearby area settlers of European ancestry called Agua Fria.

The Chaushila and Chauchila sub-tribes, although organized into different main tribes, had a similar name because both of them derived their livelihood from the same river. Today, that river, as well as a modern day tribe encompassing descendants of both groups is known as the Chowchilla. A formerly uninhabited portion of the Chaushilha tribal land is now the City of Chowchilla. Shehamniu was in between Chowchilla and an unincorporated area known as Fairmead. Another small Chaushila village, whose name no one can remember and wiped out completely before 1840, may have been located closer to what today is a farm near Avenue 26 and Road 12. There were also two other documented Chaushilha villages, one only slightly south and west of Shehamniu, the other near the modern-day city of Los Banos. This farthest west village was more deeply affected by the California mission system, and ceased to exist in the early 19th century.

The people of Shehamniu frequently visited their neighbors in the other Chaushilha villages and in Mariposa, Ahwahnee and Okhumhurst. About once a year or so, the men of the village would join with other Chaushilha to visit and trade with Native Americans from the Costanoan or Miwok tribes. The Costanoans' tribal lands extended from the hills west of the Yokut villages all the way to the Pacific Ocean. No man from Shehamniu had seen the ocean, but had learned of it in their communications with the Costanoans. Because the Costanoans had access to the ocean, they were able to bring different kinds of animals, such as seals, crabs and clams.

The Miwoks tribal areas extended north of where the Chaushilha tribe dwelt. It largely was where Yosemite National Park is now located, although the Ahwaneechee also spent time in the southern part of what is now the park. Another small portion of Miwok territory extended west to the ocean. This portion of the Miwok territory was north of the Costanoans' land, and separated from it by a large L-shaped bay we in modern times know as the San Francisco Bay. Most of the Yokut villages were southwest of the Miwok lands. The Yokut land also extended west to what is now known, especially in the modern farming industry, as the "West Side."

In 1849, California was not a state, but it was considered a territory of the United States. In 1821, Mexico had ceded control of the region to the United States. In those days, many Mexican families (most of them a mix of Spanish and Native American ancestry) were already establishing families in what was then known as "Alta California." This was mostly in what we know as Southern California, but on occasion these men would ride horses far north, primarily into the Costanoan areas but also into some of the Yokut villages west of the San Joaquin River. They would raid these villages, and they spread diseases like tuberculosis to them. Those villages were rapidly losing population, even faster than Shehamniu. Most of them did not survive into the 20th century.

The people of Shehamniu were not as severely affected in their day to day life by what was going on miles to the west of them. But, because of periodically trading with them, they knew what was happening. In fact, it was through these trading expeditions they brought back tuberculosis, which eventually killed off almost their entire village.

What the people of Shehamniu didn't know was far to the north of them, in much of the Miwoks' territory, White men and even a few White women were arriving by the thousands. These White people were forming new cities, such as Sacramento near the northern edge of the Miwoks territory, and San Francisco in the northernmost territory of the Costanoans, on the shore of the bay that divided them from the Miwoks. These new settlers were in search of gold, which the White people were using as currency. The Yokuts also had currency, beads made from seeds. They used these to trade with other tribes.

The White people were using their gold to return to their homelands and purchase things the Chaushilhas had never seen, such as spun fabric, furniture, lumber, horses and cattle. They sometimes even bought machines that could make the fabric and the furniture. Others were constructing saw mills, and cutting down the large trees in the Chauchila and Ahwaneechee tribes' areas to make even more lumber.

Meanwhile, the horses and cattle they brought from elsewhere were eating the native grasses. The White settlers would often surround their horses and cattle with wooden fences, cutting off the wild animals' access to some of their territory. With less territory, fewer animals survived. This is why, even in the Chaushilha tribal areas, which in 1849 few White men had ventured, animals were disappearing.

Within two years of gold first being discovered by one of the White men who lived near Sacramento, the leaders of all these new White settlements would declare almost 163,700 square miles to be "California." This took in 900 miles of coastline, from San Diego to the northernmost reaches of the Russian colonies, and to an area Whites had previously recognized as "Oregon Territory." The boundaries of California extended east to two large lakes, Goose Lake to the north and Lake Tahoe some 250 miles south. From Lake Tahoe, the new eastern boundary took in areas increasingly further east until crossing the Colorado River about 230 miles north of Mexico. Along those 230 miles, the river served as California's eastern boundary.

The new settlers of California relayed messages back to Washington, D.C. saying all people in California wanted to join the United States of America. With that communication and a vote of White men from lands much further away from Shehamniu than its residents could possibly have imagined, California became the 31st state in the United States of America on Sept. 9, 1850.

These new settlers had never asked the Yokuts, the Miwoks, the Costanoans, nor any of the other Native American tribes in California for their opinions. The Chauchila and Ahwaneechee tribal leaders had given their opinions anyhow. When they saw White settlers building homes of lumber, brick and mortar in their tribal lands, they asked the newcomers to leave. The Whites refused to do so.

Most of the White settlers considered the reddish-skinned people they encountered "out west" to be savages. That at times seemed an accurate description of the Chaushilha and Chauchila tribes, whose men typically had a fiercer, more warlike spirit than others. Elsewhere though, most of the natives were peaceful. They at first approached the Whites as they would any other strangers, using sign language to offer their baskets, leather goods and rafts for things the White people had. Sometimes the Native Americans were able to form friendships and trade goods with the new people, but often the White men captured the natives – men, women and children. They forced their captives onto reservations dozens or more miles away from their home villages. Sometimes, they even sold the Indian children as slaves, although a condition of being admitted to the United States was that Californians not have slaves.

CHAPTER 2

The men of Shehamniu were still completely unaware of these things that had happened over the previous two years when they decided to again go hunting on Dec. 17, 1850. All they knew is after more than a year of being able to find food on their own land, the meat supply had once again become scarce. As they had 13 months before, most of them headed in their rafts up the river to where it split the two plateaus. Achachak, Kajika and Wahchinksapa headed along the south bank on horseback, trying to keep the horses from bolting ahead of the rafts.

This time, they were surprised to see what seemed to be about 1,000 men on the south bank. Some were Ahwaneechee, others Chauchila. Some of the men were on horseback, just like three of their own. Tenaija, the Ahwaneechee chief, gestured further south. The Chaushilhas wondered if they were planning a trading expedition with the Chukchansi, or if he was warning them of something more serious.

When Chief Tenaija saw Achachak, Kajika and Wahchinksapa, he immediately recognized the animals they were riding. "Hey you Chaushilhas, where did you get those horses?" he yelled as they came within hearing distance. He spoke all the words except "horses" in Yokutsan. Since there was no word for the animals in their native language, Chief Tenaija used the same word as the White settlers who had already made their way into his area.

"Horses? How did you know that's what they are called? Until just now, we had never seen any animals like these but our three!" yelled Chief Red Hawk, as both horses and rafts came closer to the army of neighboring tribes.

"Put your rafts under the oak trees and I'll tell you what's going on," Chief Tenaija replied. "But first, have you seen any of the pale-faced men?"

"No, I haven't seen any ghosts," said Chief Red Hawk.

"Not ghosts. Real men," Chief Tenaija explained. "They look a lot like us, but their skin is much paler. Their hair is short. And these horses are only a few of the strange things they have. Plus, not too many of them are nice."

Chief Tenaija then explained to the Chaushilhas how a year or two before, a White man who called himself Jim Savage had established something he called a store near one of the other rivers running through Ahwaneechee land. Savage kept many things in the store, such as food like the Ahwaneechee had never seen previously, blankets, and sharp tools. In exchange for pieces of gold, he let a few other White people, both men and women, take these things. Ahwaneechee also traded feathers and their women's baskets for these. In exchange for one of Chief Tenaija's own daughters, Savage had given him six horses and one steer.

What's more, three young single men from the Ahwaneechee tribe worked with Savage at the store, and he had given them everything they needed. This included the right to sleep in a building next to the store. But, two moons before, Savage had locked up the store and headed west through Miwok territory.

"We need more blankets, and we need more food," Chief Tenaija said. "But the three men who work there will not open the store. They told me Savage ordered them not to let anyone in while he was gone."

"We need food too!" said Chief Red Hawk. "That's why we came up to the plateau!"

"I have discussed this with Chief Jose Rey from the Chauchila tribe," said Chief Tenaija. He has many pale-face people settling near his village. The animals have been disappearing from the area, so it is harder for his men to find adequate meat for their families. But Savage usually has one entire wall full, because he keeps slaughtering these other animals he brought with him. They're called cattle, but he calls their meat beef. It's very tasty.

"Our plan is we will head down to the store. There are some openings in the walls, although they are covered with a strange surface. It's completely clear, but it keeps the bugs out. It is thin. I think we can break the clear openings and get what he has in the store."

"Let's do it!" Chief Red Hawk replied. With that order, the men and a few Chaushilha boys like Wabakashiek began their trek from their boundary down to Okumhurst, the Ahwaneechee Village where Chief Tenaija and his men lived. It was dark, so the men joined the women, children and elders of the Ahwaneechee village for dinner, and settled themselves around the campfire in the middle of the ring of Ahwaneechee wiki-ups.

 The next morning, they were joined by a few more men from Ahwahnee, another Ahwaneechee village, and made their way down the trail to Savage's store. The Chaushilhas had never seen anything like this. There were three buildings. Instead of curving willow twigs and tying them with tules from the river, Savage's buildings were constructed from large, flat and smooth pieces of wood. On top of each, smaller wood pieces lay in an interlocking and sloping pattern, forming a peak at the top of each building. As Chief Tenaija had explained, two of the three buildings appeared to have openings on the sides.

"We're going to the large building closest to the trail," Chief Tenaija told all of the travelers. "But watch out for the building without the windows. That is where the three men who work in his store are staying. If they are in their building, all they have to do is hear the commotion and poke their head out the door, then they will see us. Savage also has a device he calls a gun, which shoots out these weird things he calls bullets. He's never proven it, but he says it takes only one bullet to kill a man. If his men see us trying to break into the store, they may have his bullets, and they may try to use them on us."

Quickly, all the assembled Native Americans surrounded the store. Some of the Ahwaneechees and Chauchila had tools the Chaushilhas had never seen before. These tools had long pieces of wood, like branches, but smooth. Attached to the smooth branches was something that looked like a rock with one sharp edge. But, while the "rock" was black, the sharp edge was a shiny color the Chauchila had never seen before.

"Take the axes to the windows! Break the glass" Chief Tenaija barked.

With that, the men with the long-handled tools smashed the clear surface covering each of the openings in the walls. When they had broken openings large enough for a grown man to enter, the axe wielders jumped into the store, followed by some of their fellow tribesmen. The Chaushilhas quickly followed behind them, including Wabakashiek.

"Damn!" said Chief Tenaija, in English since there were no swear words in Yokutsan. "He took all the meat, and the produce!"

Wabakashiek looked around. One whole wall and another short wall with similar openings to what Chief Tenaija had called windows were empty. There were also many smooth pieces of wood inside. Although smaller, some were standing almost as tall as the room on their narrow edges. Others were wedged between the tall pieces so the long edges faced the floor or the ceiling. There were five pieces of wood lying down between each of the tall pieces, and there were also pieces lying down on the top and bottom between each two pieces of wood that were standing up. Throughout the store, there were six of these structures with two pieces of wood standing, seven lying down. On each lying down piece of wood except the ones at the top, there were shiny objects, round but flat on top.

He noticed another wall filled with some material made of bright colors and many different patterns. Each different piece of material looked somewhat like the deerskin Aunt Macha and the other women had fashioned into loincloths for him, Papa and the other men. Chaushilha women had painted designs on their loin clothes with dyes made from fresh berries, uncured acorn flesh and the leaves of trees. They did likewise with the longer deerskin garments the women and girls wore. But these materials on the wall were different. They looked as if the colors and patterns were part of the material, and their color was brighter than anything he'd seen before.

As beautiful as the material was, something else quickly caught Wabakashiek's eye. He noticed one of the round objects on the flat stacked wood in the middle of the room had a picture of blackberries, just like the ones he'd picked with Aunt Macha sometimes. He picked the can up.

Chief Tenaija saw Wabakashiek pick up the can of blackberries, and went over to one of the far shelves. He came back with another shiny tool, all of it sparkling like the edges of the axes they'd used to break the windows. This tool, about as long as Chief Tenaija's big hands, had two long handles on one end, and two shorter ones on the other end.

Chief Tenaija took the can from Wabakashiek's hand. He placed the tool on the can so that the two short handles were centered on the edge. The Ahwaneechee chief squeezed the long handles with one hand while turning the short handles. This caused the tool to move alongside the edge of the can. To Wabakashiek's surprise, the top edge of this thing with the blackberries on it began to pull away from the sides! Once Chief Tenaija had completely removed the top part of the blackberry thing, he gave it back to Wabakashiek.

"Be careful young man. The edge is sharp. Don't let the can's edges cut you," the chief told him.

Wabakashiek looked inside the open circle, and saw the rest was filled with blackberries.

"How did they get in here?" he asked the chief. "Are they good to eat?"

"All these cans have inside whatever the picture on the outside shows," Chief Tenaija said. Most of them are things you have never seen before. Even these blackberries aren't quite the same as the ones that grow on your lands. But yes, they are all good. Can I have one of your blackberries?"

"Sure!" Wabakashiek replied.

Chief Tenaija took one of the blackberries out of the can and ate it. Seeing the Ahwaneechee chief's smile, Wabakashiek took another one out and ate it. It was softer than any blackberry he had ever tasted before. It was not quite as flavorful as the ones he and Aunt Macha had harvested from the vines in summer time. But summer had been a long time ago, and they'd had nothing but dried berries, raisins, acorn bread, acorn mush and rabbits for quite some time.

"That's good! Thank you Chief Tenaija! Papa, you want some?" His father took one and ate. Realizing there was no way to safely transport them back to where they'd left the rafts, Wabakashiek and Tashi began eating more of the open can of blackberries, fully intending to devour the entire contents of the can right then and there.

As they ate, they noticed some of the other men were knocking the cans to the floor and wrapping them unopened in thick pieces of cloth. Other men were throwing all kinds of shiny tools off the shelves in the back of the room, and onto other thick pieces of cloth. They seemed in a hurry.

"What's the rush Chief Tenaija?" Tashi asked.

"If the men who work in the store come back, there could be trouble!" the chief replied.

A few minutes later, Wabakashiek (and everyone else) bristled at the sound of footsteps.

"Hey! What's going on up there?!" they heard a voice shouting from outside the store.

The men who had broken the windows with the axes picked them back up and jumped out the windows, heading back up the hill they had come down. So did six of the men who were in the back of the store, each of them carrying axes that had previously been locked in the store. These axes were even shinier than the ones the others had been carrying. Many of the other men followed out the windows.

Wabakashiek and the other young boys tried to join them. But all of the fathers of the less than full-grown boys were holding back. This included Tashi. As Wabakashiek lifted his foot, intending to jump through the now smashed out window, Tashi grabbed his hand.

"There's only three of them and plenty of us. You and I, plus the other men and boys still here, are going to guard this stuff!" Tashi told his son. "So get down, and don't even look out that window."

Bemo, Lansa and Sahale, the three Ahwaneechee who lived on James Savage's property, had just returned from bear hunting in the high country. When they saw the dozens of fellow Native Americans jumping from the broken windows of the store they had promised Savage they would protect, fear struck them. They had taken bows and arrows, but not the three guns Savage had left with them. Those were still in the barn.

Savage's men knew they had to do something quickly. But how could they fend off the intruders when it had taken five arrows to kill the bear they'd found up in the high country? They only had about two dozen arrows left between them. What good would that do against dozens of men? They knew if they didn't stop these intruders, Savage would probably kill them when he returned.

So they dropped the bear they were carrying, and began loading arrows into bows. But it was too late. Three quick, intruders ran with their axes to Bemo, Lanse and Sahale and planted each into the backs of their heads. Bemo, Lanse and Sahale quickly fell to the ground, dead.

Wabakashiek was horrified by what he saw, and couldn't hold back the tears. Tashi had never seen even one man killed before either, so he wasn't angry with his son. He was worried.

"No time for crying, Wabakashiek," he said. "We've got to get out of this place now!"

But, as they and the other men and boys tried to jump out the windows, they noticed every man who didn't have an axe was coming back down the hill. This included Chief Jose Rey of the Chauchila. Meanwhile, the men with axes, including Chief Tenaija and their own Chief Red Hawk, were taking them to the already-dead bear Bemo, Lanse and Sahale had been carrying.

"What's going on?" Tashi said to Chapa, one of the returning Chaushilha tribesmen.

"Chief Tenaija said it's safe to get the goods," Chapa said. "You men and boys grab as much as you can, including some of that fabric in the corner. Then go up to the dead bear by the dead men."

By this time, Wabakashiek and Tashi had eaten the entire can of blackberries, and had thrown more cans of many different kinds of food down onto the blanket by them. With the help of the other Chaushillha tribesmen who were there, they picked up corners and sides of the blanket and carried them up the hill. Other groups followed, some of them taking the colorful material down from the walls, some of them grabbing more of the shiny tools on the other side of the room.

They walked with all of these goods up to the dead men. The men with the axes had hacked the bear into pieces. The men who had taken the colorful material began unwinding it. Wabakashiek hadn't realized the material was actually rolled onto a large, white object. Unwound, it was much thinner than the deerskin everyone he knew wore.

A man who had been taking the tools out produced one that looked like two sticks with big knotholes on each end. That's the closest thing Wabakashiek could think of that looked like the scissors he was seeing. He was amazed that sticks with knotholes could be made so smooth, so straight, so shiny. The man spread the two sticks simply by putting his right thumb in one knothole and his forefinger in the other, and lightly flicking the knotholes apart. With his left hand, he positioned the thin, colorful material between the two spread open sticks, then squeezed the knotholes back together. The two sticks came together so tightly Wabakashiek could hear the material scrunching between them. This caused a piece of the material to come apart from what was still rolled onto the fabric bolt. When the man had completely removed it from the other material, he handed it to one of his tribesmen.
The other man picked up several pieces of the dead bear, wrapped them in the material and handed them to Chief Red Hawk.

"Thank you for helping us break into the store," Chief Tenaija said. "Enjoy some meat after all. Take your share of the cans of food and the tools. Then it is best you head back to the plateau and down the other river, so you can be home by dark. We will deal with Savage when he comes back to our village."

After the Chaushilhas left, the Chauchila and Ahwaneechee men hauled the bodies of the dead men into the store. Then they lit the store on fire. This would keep them warmer. They hoped it would also destroy the evidence of what had happened.

They spent the night there, waiting for the fire to burn the bodies to embers, and for the embers to cool down sufficiently so they could be handled. Once that was accomplished, they headed with the remains of their fallen kinsmen back to their villages.

All three of the men were from Okumhurst. Their ashes were scattered there. It had been the Ahwaneechee tribe's intention to honor these men the following summer, in an annual ceremony recognizing all who had died over the past year.

The river where James' Savage's store and Okumhurst was located in later times would become known as the Fresno River. The area encompassing both the Okumhurst, and areas to the south extending way past Jim Savage's store, became known first as Fresno Flats, then as Oakhurst. In the 21st Century, Oakhurst is so large it extends clear to Ahwahnee.

Ahwahnee was also the name of a hotel that would be built in the early 20th century, in what became Yosemite National Park. Yosemite had been one of the Miwok chiefs. The park was so large, it stretched from just north of the Ahwaneechee villages into territories of the Miwok tribe far north. With modern-day Mariposa being on the border of what is now known as the Chowchilla River, the ancient boundary between Yokuts and Miwoks, that community can call itself the ancestral home of both tribes. Yosemite is located almost entirely in Miwok territory, not only bordering Yokut lands on the north and west, but also spreading through Miwok territory to the boundaries they shared with Monache, Paiute and Shoshone tribes.

CHAPTER 3

Sure enough, when James Savage returned to his compound on Jan. 10, 1851 he was deeply disturbed by what he saw. The store had been broken into, the windows smashed, the walls a charcoaled ruin. Everything in it was gone, and so were his workers.

The entire San Joaquin Valley and central California foothills, clear to the boundaries with modern day Los Angeles and other southern California counties, had been designated "Mariposa County" when California became a state. Agua Fria, a White settlement two miles west of the traditional Native American village of Mariposa, was the county seat in 1850. This meant James Savage had a day's ride to Agua Fria.

When Savage reported the crime to Sheriff James Burney, both knew whom to suspect. It had to have been the Ahwaneechee villagers just north of Savage's camp. They rounded up a posse of other White men and the next morning headed for Okumhurst.

"Do you boys know anything about what happened at Jim Savage's store?" Sheriff Burney asked Chief Tenaija when the posse arrived in Okumhurst.

"Today is the first time we have seen Jim Savage in over three moons," Chief Tenaija replied.

"I don't like that answer. Now, do you or do you not know what happened at the store while he was gone?" Burney asked, in an angrier tone of voice.

"I don't like you calling us boys," Chief Tenaija replied. "Burney, I am probably old enough to be your father. My family has lived here for generations. We did ask your people to leave, because Savage and all the rest of you people are taking up too much space. Savage's compound alone is bigger than the entire village of Okumhusrt!"

"And it's about to get smaller," Sheriff Burney shouted, motioning for the posse to draw their guns.

But, on the hill above where Sheriff Burney and Chief Tenaija had this conversation, other members of the Ahwaneechee tribe were ready with their bows and arrows, as well as the guns they had taken from the store last month. As soon as they saw the posse draw their guns, Chief Tenaija's oldest son, Nootau, let one arrow sail. He was a skilled hunter, and was able to land that arrow just south of where his father and Sheriff Burney had their confrontation.

"Ok, I see you were ready for us," Sheriff Burney said. "I'm not going to risk getting this entire posse killed. But you Injuns are the problem, not us. I'm going to appeal to the governor to organize an entire battalion to get rid of you. Be ready for reservation life!"

Although White men had generally lived in peace near the Native villages, not everyone got along. As in any community, there were occasional conflicts between people, and there were some men, both White and Native, who had stolen from other people, gotten into physical altercations and even raped women. Occasionally, even young women got into trouble. Unfortunately, a disproportionate number of these law-breakers were Native American.

The previous April, before California was admitted into the United States, the state legislature had passed the Act for Government and Protection of Indians. It gave all people in the state the right to bring complaints to their local law enforcement officials. Their cases would be investigated and tried by jury. But, even in cases of murder or rape, a Native American could not allege wrong doing by a White person if the only witnesses were other Natives. The Act also allowed the United States government to revoke the Native American's rights to their tribal lands, including the villages where they lived, if local law enforcement deemed this necessary. This would force the Natives off their own historic tribal lands.

Sheriff James Burney had not wanted to destroy the Native American villages under his tenure as the first sheriff of Mariposa County. As he saw it, it was possible for the two groups to live peacefully. Yet, he could not understand Native American customs and beliefs. It appeared to him these sometimes were the root of conflicts between them and the White settlers. As he saw it, the White settlers were within their rights to establish homes on the uninhabited portions of Mariposa County, just as he had done in Agua Fria in 1849 when he came prospecting for gold.

The sheriff had attained the rank of major with the U.S. Army before coming to California. As a young man, he had fought in the War of 1812. He saw firsthand how the Native Americans in the original 13 colonies had no allegiance to the United States, and worked with the British to prevent American expansion to the west. Unlike the European Loyalists he knew in those days, it wasn't that the eastern United States Native American tribes felt any allegiance to Great Britain. They just took advantage of the enemy troops to try and achieve their own desires.

Now, it seemed to Sheriff Burney, the tribes he was dealing with in California were not looking to the interests of their country either. Instead, just like the eastern tribes, they were more concerned with their own selfish interests. The attack on James Savage's store, and the disappearance of the three Ahwaneechee men who worked there was proof. The Natives would even kill their own people to get what they wanted, and they had to be stopped. This is why he wrote an appeal to the governor of California. He requested the governor organize a militia to remove all of the known Mariposa County tribes to somewhere else.

What Sheriff Burney had not known then was two days before his skirmish with the Ahwaneechee, California's first governor, Peter Burnett, had resigned. This followed growing tensions with the state legislature over how non-Europeans, including Native Americans, were treated. Lt. Governor John McDougall had taken over the governorship.

Burnett had favored exterminating all Native Americans, but had compromised with the Legislature to keep the pre-admission act in place. McDougall favored a more moderate approach to dealing with the Natives. But, when he received Sheriff James Burney's appeal in mid-January, 1851 the new governor still needed time to evaluate his position.

At the same time, the federal government was pursuing a less hostile approach. It wanted to "domesticate" the Native Americans, that is, reserve certain portions of an area for them, and allow the Whites to fully colonize other areas. Since Burnett had not been receptive to this idea, the Bureau of Indian Affairs had not made any headway on this approach when McDougall assumed the governorship.

Ultimately, McDougall decided to organize a militia against the Mariposa County tribes. He put the crime victim James Savage, who had also obtained the rank of major in the United States Army, in charge of the militia. Serving as captains under Major Savage were Mariposa County settlers John J. Kuykendall, John Boling and Richard Dill. Each captain managed a battalion going to a different part of the then-sprawling Mariposa County.

McDougall delayed deployment of this militia because the federal government preferred a less violent approach. It wanted to negotiate treaties with the Native American tribes, in which the Natives would give up their tribal lands in exchange for horses, cattle and advisors to help them cultivate other lands. One of these reservations was Camp Barbour, nearer to Agua Fria than to the Native American village in Mariposa. On March 19, 1851 representatives of a special commission met at Camp Barbour with tribal leaders from six tribes, and negotiated a treaty with them. The militia Governor McDougall had assembled also was present for this treaty summit.

Tribes present were the Costonoans, Miwoks, Chukchansi, Monache, Paiutes and residents of the Ahwahnee village of the Ahwaneechee tribe. These tribes once inhabited an area ranging from San Francisco on the west, the southern San Joaquin Valley on the south, Mono Lake on the east and all of the area that would later be incorporated into Yosemite National Park on the north. This treaty was one of 18 the commission negotiated with Native American tribes. It required the southern members of these tribes to relocate to Camp Barbour, and the others to relocate to an area along the Tuolumne River.

Noticeably absent from the peace treaty summit were the tribal leaders of two tribes smack in the middle – members of the Ahwaneechee tribe living in the Okhumhurst village, and anyone from the Chauchila tribe. Since Chauchila and Chaushilha are pronounced identically in English, neither the commissioners negotiating the treaty, nor any of the other White settlers were aware a separate tribe lived on the San Joaquin Valley floor. But they were aware of the Natives living in Okhumhurst and Mariposa. There were also several other tribes in what was then the southern reaches of Yokut territory that had not signed. The White settlers were furious about this.

"Ok men. We're going to have to take the Ahwaneechee from Fresno Flats, the Chauchila, and Kaweah tribes by force," Major James Savage told his militia. "So here's the plan. Captain Kuykendall's men will head south to capture the Kaweah. They'll be taken to a reservation on their river. Captains Boling and Dill will head north with me. We'll capture the Ahwaneechee first, and half our division will take them to Camp Barbour. The rest of our army will then head to Mariposa, and we will reunite in Fresno. From there we will make sure no Yokuts are camping on the valley floor. All Indians will be in custody or dead!"

The Yokut tribal lands actually extended about 80 miles south and somewhat west of Shehamniu. Thus, it was Capt. Kuykendall who found the first Yokut village, Choimini, on the bank of the Kings River. His battalion charged the village, killing several of its young warriors, and capturing most of the rest of that village. A few Choimini residents escaped and headed north, seeking safety in exchange for the warning of the U.S. Army battalion's intrusion onto their tribal lands.

As they headed north, warning each village of the impending danger, many of the village chiefs were afraid the White people's faster horses, superior weapons and well-organized militia tactics would be too much for their warriors. It wouldn't be worth it, even if the entire tribe mounted an attack, to risk annihilation over relocation to the foothills. And so, before even making it up to the villages of Picayune, Halua and Shehamniu, a delegation of the southern Yokut headed up to the reservation at Camp Barbour, ready to surrender. Others from the southern villages continued north to tell the Picayune, Halau and Shehamniu villagers what was happening.

Meanwhile, on March 27, 1851, Captains Boling and Dill headed with their battalions to Okhumhurst. They chased the Ahwaneechees there up to the tribe's third village, Wawona, located midway between a grove of tall trees and Yosemite Valley. The militia battled rain, sleet and snow on the chase to Wawona, but found very few of the Ahwaneechee there. Except for a few elderly full-time residents of Wawona, most of the tribe had run all the way into the snowy high country. They were making plans to camp at one of the lakes far above the Yosemite Valley floor. The lake they were headed to is now known as Lake Tenaya, an attempt by White men of the late 19th century to honor the chief who had so gallantly fought the early California pioneers. The battalions, unable to find enough Natives to justify a trip all the way down to Camp Barbour, retreated to their settlement next to Okhumhusrt. There, they made plans to go after the Chauchila in Mariposa.

While the Kuykendall battalion, its captives and the southern Yokut delegation were heading to Camp Barbour, and the Boling and Dill battalions were chasing the Ahwaneechee, the rest of the southern Yokuts rounded up the Picayune and Halau residents and headed to Shehamniu. Under the leadership of Shehamniu's Chief Red Hawk, the Chaushila tribe had developed itself into a mighty army, and its warriors weren't so quick to give in. Instead, they convinced the southern warriors to head up Mariposa ready to fight. They were there when Major James Savage's two battalions arrived in Mariposa on April 13, 1851.

A fierce battle ensued in Mariposa. It began when the battalions spotted a larger number than usual of Native Americans in Mariposa. They charged down the mountain into this village, firing rifles and shotguns. The Native Americans immediately began defending themselves, both with bows and arrows and the guns they had started to accumulate.

About 100 Native Americans and some 25 men from Major Savage's battalions died that day. While some of the dead were Chaushilha warriors, most of them decided to escape back down the hill, making it safely to Shehamniu before nightfall. Survivors from Shehamniu and a few of the other villages continued life as usual, although obstacles throughout the rest of the 19th century made it increasingly difficult.

The Chauchila did not fare as well, since there wasn't a village to which they could escape. Furthermore, the Chauchila had started following the White settler's example, storing dried meat, seeds and acorn powder in a community hut, doling it out to all Mariposa families in the winter months. The battalions destroyed this "store," leaving the entire village with inadequate food, and too few people capable of finding more. What's more Chief Jose Rey was gravely wounded, and did not survive the night.

With their chief dead and everyone else at risk of starvation, the Chauchila tribe decided it was time to move away from Mariposa, and begin a new life at Camp Barbour. The next morning, a delegation of Chauchila traveled from Mariposa to Agua Fria, surrendering to the militia at their camp by Sheriff James Burney's cabin.

This left only the Ahwaneechee to capture. The militia, including Captain Kuykendall's men, headed back up to Wawona, figuring the younger and healthier residents would come back and take care of the old people they'd seen there in March. This proved to be correct. Several Ahwaneechee men did return to Wawona Village on May 22, 1851 to provide their elders with fresh meat. The militia, hiding on the hill below Wawona, observed the Natives, and followed them to their camp at what is now known as May Lake. There they captured and forced the Ahwaneechee to surrender and accept reservation life.

CHAPTER 4

Since Wabakashiek was only 11 years old in 1851, he did not go with the men of his village to fight in the Mariposa War. Since the teenage boys of his village did accompany their fathers to war, Wabakashiek was the oldest male left in the village, except for the tribal elders. He therefore felt some responsibility to protect his people when Raymond "Ralph" Eastman showed up and began chopping a tree down on the bank of the Chowchilla River opposite their village.

Nor did Wabakashiek harbor the fear and hatred for White men those older than him now felt. In spite of his exposure to European culture on the hunting trips he had gone on in 1849 and 1850, Eastman was still the first White man Wabakashiek had ever seen. To the boy, it seemed this blond-haired blue-eyed man wasn't human, but some kind of spirit. A good one, he hoped. Wabakashiek heard the screech of a hawk above, and took that as a sign of the bird's approval. It may actually have been a warning.

"Hey Redskin boy!" Eastman said, smiling at Wabakashiek as he came up the hill to the bank on his side of the river.

"Me Wabakashiek!," the young man replied. "That's our tree!"

Eastman didn't really believe the common sentiment that Indians were savages. He believed they would gladly work on the wheat farm he would plant. In turn, he planned to make sure they had adequate food and clothing, and their children would receive education in the ways of civilized people.

Eastman, with his wife and two children, had arrived in California by covered wagon during the 1849 Gold Rush, staking a claim in Sonora. After two years, he'd had little success in mining, and his money was running low. In April, 1851, when the snow melted in Sonora, he headed due south on his horse, with only a compass, a tiny amount of food and two bags of wheat he carried in saddlebags. He ended up at the Chowhilla River's north side, opposite the village of Shehamniu. Here, he made plans to plant the bags of wheat on the flat terrain.

Wabakashiek didn't speak a word of English when he laid eyes on Eastman. The newcomer, however, had learned to speak some of the very similar Miwok language spoken by Native Americans in Sonora. He understood why the boy who had just identified himself as Wabakashiek was concerned.

"I'm Mr. Eastman," he told the young man. I'm cutting these branches so I can live here too. Then I'll plant wheat in this field, enough for me, you and the whole village!" Other than the gestures Eastman made, pointing to himself, then Wabakashiek and then to the village, the boy didn't understand. Eastman picked up his axe and finished chopping the tree down.

"Hey, give me a hand here," Eastman said, gesturing toward the stump, when the tree fell to the ground.

Wabakashiek, not understanding, stood over the cut tree. He wondered why Eastman had not just broken off the branches he would need to build his wiki-up. Then, down the north bank, he noticed the canvas tent Eastman had erected as his own temporary lodging. "What did he need the tree for at all?" Wabakashiek wondered silently. Nevertheless, he went over to the stump where Eastman was standing. Eastman placed the trunk in the boy's hands, then walked over to the leafy side of the tree and grabbed one branch. He then started walking down the bank, pulling the tree trunk out of Wabakashiek's hand.

"I need you to hold this tree!" he shouted to the boy. He went back up to the bank, and picked up the tree trunk again. "Hold it right here!"

This time, Wabakashiek understood and helped Eastman carry the tree down the bank. There, Eastman cut the branches off with his axe, and split the trunk into two long pieces. He then took his pocket knife, and used its blade to smooth one side of each log. Once they were smooth, he tied both logs with ropes to the harness of his horse. Eastman began leading the horse to drag the logs, so that they would unearth the grass from the soil beneath them. Since it was spring, and the valley receives sufficient rainfall, the grass easily left the ground.

Wabakashiek stayed with Eastman, watching this strange behavior. Once Eastman had cleared about 40 acres of grass, he got off the horse and began throwing the clumps of unearthed grass into piles at the edge of his new field. He gestured to Wabakshiek, and when the boy came up to him, put a clump of grass in his hand. Wabakashiek threw it way beyond the pile Eastman had started.

"That's a good throw, Redskin," Eastman said. "But your arm will get tired if you keep throwing like that. Do it this way." Eastman picked up some more clumps of grass and gently tossed them onto the pile he was creating. Wabakashiek copied him until the field was free of grass. Then, Eastman picked up one of the two bags of wheat he had stored under one of the trees on the river, and carried it back up to the field. He opened a corner of the bag, grabbed a handful of wheat seeds, and began scattering them in one row near the edge of the field.

Wabakashiek also grabbed a handful of seed, and accepted Eastman's direction to scatter them in a second row three feet away from the first one. They repeated this process with all of the first bag and half of the second, until the entire field was planted. By this time the sun was low on the western horizon.

"You'd better go back to your village now, Redskin," Eastman said. "Now that I have this wheat planted, I need you to keep an eye on it while I go on a journey."

With that, Eastman went into his tent. Wabakashiek went back across the river to Shehamniu. As he had almost every day of his life, he enjoyed a meal of acorn bread with acorn mush, then listened to the tribal elders tell stories. Wabakashiek wanted to tell a story too. But he was afraid the elders would not believe he had seen a god-like man, and even if they did believe it, would be mad at both of them for taking all the grass out of the field across the river.

The next morning, Eastman headed back up the hill to begin the week-long ride to Sonora. He wanted to bring his wife Clara and his two young children, Eliza and John, down to the farm he had just established. But there was much he still had to do before he could. Thankfully, in 1851 a wheat field planted next to a river would pretty much grow on its own. Eastman thought he would just have to come back and harvest the crop a few months later.

The San Joaquin Valley floor, south of the San Francisco Bay at least, was still largely untouched by White settlers in the early 1850s. But communities in between San Francisco and Sacramento were rapidly growing, and had incorporated as cities soon after California became a state. This was even true of Sonora, where Eastman had been able to quickly acquire lumber and other supplies to build a nice home for his family on arrival.

But now, he'd have to do this all over again, and it wouldn't be nearly as easy. First, he had to figure out a way to haul all those supplies down the steep Sierra Nevada Mountains to the field. Then he would have to figure out how to haul his family down the mountains. He was sure the route he had taken on horseback was too steep, so he would have to figure out a different way to go back.

First and foremost, he'd have to make some money. Gold mining had been so disastrous for him, he didn't have enough money to buy the supplies for another home, nor to purchase a covered wagon and team of oxen.

Eastman figured the river he had just established his farm on would lead, somehow, back to the Bay Area. In actuality, the Chowchilla River feeds into the San Joaquin River near the modern-day small town of Dos Palos, which in 1851 was mostly slightly swampy wilderness. The San Joaquin River then flows northwest to the San Francisco Bay.

This is the way Eastman traveled on his return to Sonora. It was a much less direct route, and difficult to cross the swampy confluence of the Chowchilla, Merced and San Joaquin rivers. Still, with flat terrain the whole way, he managed to reach the San Joaquin River by nightfall, and Stockton three days later. The next morning, he headed uphill from Stockton to Sonora. With hills being considerably steeper on that journey, even though the roads there were more well-established, it took him another two days to reach Sonora.

He reached Sonora by dinner time. Clara had prepared beans with ham, which she served with a loaf of sourdough bread and some tender artichokes that were growing wild on the property. It was the first good meal he'd had in five days.

"Clara, I have planted a wheat field a three-day journey south of here," Eastman told his wife. "Getting there was tough, as I went down a mountain no wagons would be able to traverse. But coming back to Sonora, I found another way along the river. It takes a week on horseback, and I think by wagon might take even longer. So, tomorrow, I will find work either here or in Stockton. This summer, I will go back to my field to harvest the wheat, and I will take with me the supplies to build us a decent home. Once I harvest the wheat I will come back to Sonora for all of you, and we will all go down to the farm and live there."

"As you wish," Clara replied.

She wasn't really sure she wanted to go on another covered wagon trip just two years after coming all the way from St. Louis, Missouri in 1849. Even in Sonora, there were not the comforts of home, such as fine china, abundant fresh fruits and vegetables and paved streets to walk on. Life in Sonora was decent, because there were stores and a sense of community. How would life be where they were the only people for miles around?

But, husbands didn't really ask their wife's opinions in 1851. They told them how it would be. A wife's job was to accept and help as she could.

"There is one more thing I should tell you," Eastman said. "Across the river from our field there is an Indian village. I've only talked to one young boy there; he was probably about 12 years old. He helped me grade and plant the field. For some reason I didn't see any others, just their huts. But I'm hoping that boy and the ones older than him will help me create a big operation. And I'm hoping you can teach the Indian children."

"Indians? Teach?" Clara wasn't thrilled about this idea. On the wagon train out, the Cherokee Indians had surrounded them and demanded money. But one of the men had worked for the Bureau of Indian Affairs in St. Louis. He was able to placate the men by offering them flour and tobacco. Maybe, since they were growing wheat already, that would work here.

"We'd probably better grow tobacco too," she said.

"No, tobacco won't grow in California's climate," Eastman replied. "But you're right, I should bring some with me when I go back this summer. Some milled flour too, for their women-folk."

The men of Shehamniu arrived back to their village a day after Eastman left. As they paddled their rafts around the last bend before reaching Shehamniu, they were shocked to see dirt where there had been grass before on the north side of the river. They also noticed a tree cut down on that side.

Tashi was especially concerned. He didn't think his own son would do something so foolish. Yet, the other children would not have had the physical strength necessary. How, for that matter, did Wabakashiek cut an oak tree down? Tashi had taken the only axe Wabakashiek would have been able to get his hands on easily. Had one of his fellow warriors left his axe at home? Had a younger child found it? Still, how would a younger child been able to swing the axe with enough coordination to chop down an oak tree? It had to have been Wabakashiek!

He quickly paddled to the shore, secured his raft and ran up to the village. He saw Wabakashiek and his cousins helping Macha prepare acorn loafs near their wiki-ups. Having come to the conclusion Wabakashiek was the only boy in the village strong enough to have caused the damage, he was furious with his son.

"Wabakashiek! Follow me!" Tashi demanded. As the two walked back towards the river, Tashi inquired "What happened on the other side of the river?"

Wabakashiek figured it wasn't a good idea to lie to his own father. So, he told the truth, at least as he saw it.

"A god came two days ago," Wabakashiek responded. "He cut the tree down. He cut the tree into pieces, then tied the two biggest pieces to his horse, and took out all the grass. Then we planted seeds from a brown bag all over that dirt. I can show you some proof across the river."

Tashi figured he knew what this god really was. It was a White man, just like the ones they had seen in Mariposa. The man probably had decided the property across the river now belonged to him. Fear replaced his anger.

"What exactly did this god look like, Wabakashiek?" he asked.

"He was really tall," the boy said. "He had very light skin, very light hair, lighter than our horses' hair even, and blue eyes. He wore strange clothes that covered him from the neck all the way down, and all of his arms and legs. He even had some kind of covering on his feet. "

"That wasn't a god, Wabakashiek," said Tashi. "That was a White man. And they are dangerous! If he comes back, stay away from him!"

"No Papa, he was nice. He called the seeds wheat. I think wheat might be good to eat!"

"He is not nice, he is dangerous! Stay away from him!" Tashi replied. "And since you helped him, you must be punished. Oh, I see a bunch of branches on the ground over there, I guess from the tree your "god" cut down. Go get one of those branches! Now!"

Wabakashiek went and got some of the smaller oak branches, reluctantly. Tashi decided they were too thick, so he and Wabakashiek cut them down to thin switches. Then, Wabakashiek lay on the ground, and Tashi hit him 15 times with one of the switches. Wabakashiek didn't yell or cry. He was so used to it he was able to endure the pain of being hit with an oak switch in silence.

A few days later, the field sprouted with a grass much finer than had ever grown anywhere near Shehamniu. Chief Red Hawk was the first to notice this. Kajika had been killed during the Mariposa War, so he asked Achachak, Wahchinkspa and Tashi to get the horses and walk them across the river.

"They will love that grass over there, I am sure. It looks as pristine as what I have seen in the highland meadows, in the Chauchila way-up lands," he said.

Sure enough, the horses munched at least a half- acre of the newly-planted wheat. Although the grass grew taller and thicker, the horses enjoyed their new treat every day. That is, until early summer, when the grass started sprouting heads like nothing the people of Shehamniu had ever seen. A few weeks later, that grass went from green in color to golden brown. The heads, which consisted of seeds surrounded by fine but sharp grass-like extensions, were so prickly the horses would not tolerate that sensation on their ears as they bent their necks down to graze, and would no longer eat in the field.

The people of Shehamniu thought the heads looked something like fox tails, so that is what they called the strange plants growing across the river. While the men thought it was best to burn the plants, it was Macha who came up with a better idea.

"Look how nice the seeds in the foxtails are," she said. "I believe we should harvest all these seeds, and grind them into flour with our grinding rocks. That way, we will be able to have bread before acorn season returns."

That is what the women and children of Shehamniu did. The flour these new seeds produced was much finer than acorn flour, and produced a bread with a softer texture than the acorn cakes. So, in a way, the people of Shehamniu were thankful the White man had come and planted this strange plant called wheat. Still, for those who had battled against White men in Mariposa, the one who would become their neighbor could not be trusted. As they saw it, White men were purely evil and had no business anywhere near Shehamniu.

CHAPTER 5

Eastman needed to bring many things down to his farm. He had to bring a grain cradle, so he could harvest the wheat ripening in his field. He also needed two flails, so he and a worker could thresh the seeds from the wheat. He also brought lumber to build a fence and a barn, where he would house the six oxen pulling his wagon, his horse and the wagon itself. He also had brought two more bags of wheat, so he could plant next year's crop before returning to Sonora the following spring.

Eastman also brought three shirts, a pair of pants and five pairs of breeches to fit the little boy he had met on the first trip, and three equivalent sets of clothing that would fit a small but grown man. He planned to dress the men and boys working for him in a civilized fashion. He also intended to cut their hair with scissors.

Eastman had also brought enough lumber to build the first floor of his new home. His idea had been to harvest this wheat and return to Stockton. He would then sell the wheat, purchase materials to put a second floor on the house and return to Sonora to pick up his family. They would have to sleep in a loft above the living room temporarily, but when the home was finished it would have three bedrooms upstairs.

With a heavily loaded wagon, Eastman could only travel about 10 to 15 miles each day. Since he was going downhill, the journey from Sonora to Stockton actually was the faster leg of the trip this time. Even this part took four days with an oxen-pulled covered wagon.

Intense heat slowed the oxen down even more than the level ground after they left Stockton. Eastman didn't arrive on his farm until June 30, 17 days after he had left Sonora. By this time, the residents of Shehamniu had completely harvested the field, leaving nothing but now headless wheat stalks.

"Oh my God, what have those stupid Indians done?" Eastman said when he saw the damage. "And how am I going to make it? Will my family forgive me?"

Eastman had hoped to return to his family a much wealthier man. But without a wheat crop to take with him on his next trip to Stockton, he wouldn't have the money for yet another trip by covered wagon, this time with the three most important people in his life riding inside. Instead of returning with the 1851 harvest, he would have to delay reuniting with his family by a year. That way too, he could be sure the Natives didn't steal next year's crop.

The man from Sonora was tempted to run across the river and scream at the Indians. But, as a Christian man, he felt a gentle nudging to be more forgiving. The thought also came to him that one man angrily confronting a bunch of Indians could be dangerous.

He decided to wait until after he had built a corral to secure his animals before confronting the tribe. He cut down a few oak branches, built a camp fire to roast prey he'd shot along the way that morning, and sat down between the camp fire and his tent, pitching it this time about one mile downstream from the Indian village.

The next morning, Wabakashiek and two boys only slightly younger went downstream to hunt for frogs. They had packed some of the tasty new bread for their journey, because the foxtails had yielded far more flour than a similar amount of acorns would. They also were carrying wild blackberries they had picked on a vine growing upstream from them the day before.

Summer was a hard time to find much else, especially downstream. Most of the four-legged animals were either up in the foothills, or burrowed deeply underground. Even if they weren't particularly tasty, hunting frogs was still fun. They might even be able to catch fish if they were lucky!

"Hey little Redskins, come here!" Eastman cried out to the boys when he saw them coming down the trail as he ate a bowl of oatmeal. When they turned to see who was yelling, he immediately recognized the tallest boy as William (Wabakashiek), the boy who had helped him plant the field. He barely noticed the hawk circling above the boys.

"What happened to the wheat?" he asked the boys. Wabakashiek recognized the question "Wheat?" and pulled out one of the two small loaves of bread he'd put in his knapsack. It was already a bit stained by the berries, and was not leavened like the sourdough bread Clara could make. Still, Eastman recognized it as wheat bread, something he had not eaten in more than two weeks.

"Thank you William Redskin," he said to Wabakashiek. He cut the bread into four slices with his pocket knife. After picking up one of the slices, he pointed to the other three. "You and your friends can have the rest."

It was still too early in the morning to eat again, so Wabakashiek shook his head. He also told Eastman about the warning his father had given him, slapping one hand against the other to help Eastman understand.

"You mean he hit you?" Eastman said. He hadn't completely understood the part about William's father calling White men pure evil, but it was clear the elder didn't like White men, and would punish all three of these boys now in his company if they were discovered. Eastman pondered how he would continue to benefit from the village boys' labor if their fathers would punish them for these good deeds.

These three though, were here, willing to accept further consequences. Eastman decided they should just go ahead and help him build the corral. He motioned for them to follow him to the wagon, where his fence-building supplies still were.

Guyape and Sahale had never seen oxen nor any other type of cattle up close before, so they were more interested in stroking the fur of the six creatures still yoked to the wagon. Wabakashiek had seen cows in Okhumhurst when he went there more than six months previous. He was more impressed with the stockiness of the creatures now before him.

None of the boys had ever seen a covered wagon, so Sahale lept into the back of it. Unlike Wabakashiek, Sahale had not been up to the store by Okhumhurst during the 1850 raid, so he had never seen such a wide assortment of strange new things. He jumped back out of the wagon to alert Wabakashiek and Guyape of his discovery.

"Whoa! You should see all that is in the tent on circles!" Sahale told his friends. All three boys then went into the covered wagon. Guyape, equally impressed with this assortment of things, began touching them, as did Sahale. Wabakashiek, less impressed, sat on the wagon's edge to see how Eastman would react.

"You boys don't need anything in there right now!" Eastman cried out, after he opened a sack of grain and fed his oxen. "But you can help me carry the wood."

With that, Eastman went into the wagon and began to pick up one of the 12-foot wooden posts he was carrying. Guyape and Sahale also grabbed sections of the post, so Eastman motioned for them to move it out of the wagon. Wabakashiek jumped out of the way, then grabbed a section once the others had it out of the wagon.

Eastman took the post a short distance from the wagon, then went back to get two sawhorses. The boys helped him position the pole onto the horses, and watched as Eastman grabbed a saw and a measuring tape from the wagon. He then measured and cut some of the posts into the lengths he needed to build his corral.

The design of this corral would be to erect six-foot poles every eight feet apart, and to place three eight-foot poles horizontally between each of the standing poles. The standing poles would need to be installed first, so Eastman went back into the wagon and brought out a post-hole digger.

"You guys want to try your hand with this?" Eastman asked the boys, who had accompanied him back over to the wagon, but had all three stopped to pet the oxen. As he asked, Eastman offered the post-hole digger to Wabakashiek. Wabakashiek took it from him, but not realizing how heavy it was, struggled to keep from dropping it.

"Let me help you with that, Eastman said, grabbing one pole and sliding it so that the digging end of the post-hole digger touched the ground. Wabakshiek copied him. The post-hole digger only came up to Eastman's waist, but on Wabakashiek it was chest high, and it extended to just below the other boys' necks.

Eastman steadied the post-hole digger so it was straight up and touching the ground, with Wabakashiek still holding the other end. Wabakashiek was surprised when Eastman then quickly pushed the contraption clear down into the ground, then squeezed his end to slightly widen the digger. Wabakashiek then noticed how easily the contraption disturbed the soft dirt below, making a small hole in the ground.

"Guyape, Sahale, you want to try this?" Wabakashiek asked his friends.

When Guyape grabbed one pole of the post-hole digger, Eastman walked eight paces, and pointed to the ground. As he had hoped, the two boys understood, and walked to where he was standing to dig the second hole. Eastman then walked another eight paces. Guyape and Wabakashiek dug a hole identical to the first one, albeit with a few more attempts necessary to get the post-hole digger deep enough into the ground. Eight more paces, and Guyape and Sahale gave post-hole digging a try. This was exactly what Eastman wanted. The boys, though young, were enthusiastically doing the hard work. He would just have to pace them to make sure the fence-post holes were evenly spaced.

Eastman had hauled enough fence rails to construct a 32' x 32' corral. This would provide his oxen and his horse with just under 1,000 square feet, which would be plenty considering he planned to ride the horse just about every day, and the oxen would hardly move at all. The first order of business would be to supervise the boys as they dug 16 post-holes in a square.

It took the boys and Eastman about three hours to get the post-holes down. They then moved onto Step Two, putting the short posts into the ground. Eastman went back to the stack of six-foot posts, grabbed two and walked to the post hole he had dug earlier that morning. He then leaned one of his two posts in that hole, another in the post the boys had first dug eight feet from there.

The boys understood to follow Eastman's lead, but each would only carry one post at a time. Eastman directed one boy, Wabakashiek, to put his post in the hole next to the first two, and had Guyape and Sahale follow him to the two post holes still remaining on his side, where they put the posts they were carrying. By this time, Wabakashiek was already taking the next post to its appropriate post-hole, so that left 10 to go. With a little sign language, he indicated to each boy which three post-holes he was responsible for. They had the vertical posts quickly in the right place, but each would need to be cemented into its hole.

Eastman headed back to the wagon while the boys finished delivering the posts to their correct post-holes. He grabbed a bag of cement and two metal buckets, then headed down to the river with one so he could fill it with water. The boys, as soon as they had the posts where they needed to be, ran down to join him.

"All I'm doing is filling this bucket with water, little Redskins," Eastman said as they headed back up to the wagon. "Nothing terribly exciting. You do it all the time, only with baskets instead of metal pails like mine. "

Eastman then poured some of the cement powder into the other bucket. Then he added a little water, and with a short stick he'd picked up on the river he mixed the grey substance around. Adding a little more water, he pronounced the cement done, and headed up to the fence posts with his bucket. He would personally take care of filling his 16 fence post-holes with cement, but asked one boy to hold the post as he did so.

"Very good," Eastman said. "Now, while this cement dries, we can stop for lunch. I don't know about you, but I think some more of that bread you guys brought would be good. And how about I fry the squirrels I shot yesterday?"

The boys didn't really understand what he was saying, but followed Eastman back down to the river, where he had already cut down another large oak tree the previous afternoon. This was a shock to the two younger boys, a disappointment to Wabakashiek. The Natives, for centuries, had lit fires only with the wood that had already fallen to the ground.

For Eastman, it was a necessity. It had yielded enough wood to last a month. He chopped off another branch of the fallen tree. He and the boys carried it up to the campfire ring he had made by his tent, on the other side of his wagon from the corral they were building.

Wabakashiek and his two friends watched as Eastman broke the branch into smaller pieces with his axe, then lit the campfire. The women of his village often lit campfires this early in the day if they were baking bread, but who would do it here? Digging holes was men's work. Baking bread was not. Eastman went into his tent and returned with a frying pan and the squirrels he had skinned yesterday. Without their fur, they looked simply like small pieces of pork. He placed the frying pan on the fire, then sat down next to it.

"The man is going to cook?" Wabakashiek thought to himself. "Where is his wife?" His two friends thought the same, and the whole time the squirrels were cooking, they snickered about a strong man doing the work of the women. They were also snickering because the wood was so green, it smoked terribly.

Even so, when the squirrels were done, they gladly accepted a plate of squirrel meat with the three slices of bread that had been sitting on a rock since morning. They pulled out the other loaves they had brought with them, and the wild berries, and shared these with Eastman.

After lunch, they went back to the 16 fence posts they had put in the ground. Now came the hard part. They needed to attach 48 wooden rails to the fence posts. But first, Eastman would have to split the rails. This was a skill he had learned, so the Indian boys wouldn't be able to help him. They sat back for the next two hours and watched as Eastman used a wedge and a sledge hammer to split a dozen long rails into 48 long, thin rails.

Once all the rails were split, Wabakashiek and Sahale grabbed one rail, while Guyape helped Eastman carry another to a place in between the first two fence posts they had installed earlier. Eastman had intentionally spaced the fence post a shorter distance than the rails. Six to eight feet was the recommended distance between fence posts to ensure sturdiness. Also, since he had measured the distances by pacing them out, having a longer rail would ensure that he didn't come up short if the measurement was inaccurate.

He needed the boys to hold each rail securely to the side of one fence post, and as straight as possible. To explain this, he held one of the rails to the first fence post, and motioned for Wabakashiek to come and hold it there. He guided the boy's hands to make sure it was directly perpendicular to the first fence post. He then guided Sahale to a location about one-third of the way down the rail, and Guyape to a location about two-thirds down. Motioning to make sure the boys had the rail perfectly level between the two fence posts, Eastman eyeballed how much he would need to trim from the rail, then lopped that much off with his axe. He directed the boys to lower the now approximately 8-foot rail to a location 2 ½ feet from the ground.

As he had hoped, the rail now fit securely between the two fence posts. Eastman nailed the post in at the fence post he stood by, then went over to the first fence post, where Wabakashiek was still standing.

"You want to give this a try, William Redskin?" he asked. Wabakashiek recognized "William Redskin" as the name Eastman liked to call him, and nodded yes. So, Eastman gave him the hammer and nail, then directed him as to the place where he should hammer the nail into the fence post. This came easy for Wabakashiek, and on the first try, he had completely secured the first rail between its two fence posts. They repeated the process of cutting and nailing the rails with the other one they had brought over, then grabbed two more from the pile to finish the links between the first and second post, and move on to the second and third post. It was tedious work, so by what they all recognized as "dinner time," they only had one side of the corral installed.

Since it was summer time, Eastman knew if they stopped and had a supper of canned beans, they probably could get yet another side of the corral finished before dusk. Yet, if he kept the boys from going to their village until that late, he risked the ire of their parents, which might have led to big trouble. So, once that first side was finished, he sent them back home. "It's getting late, so come back tomorrow boys," he said, pointing upstream.

The boys protested, as they had enjoyed helping Eastman build the fence. But Wabakashiek remembered the lashing his father had given him a few months before. He motioned for his friends to follow him back to the village.

Once the boys were out of sight, Eastman decided to spend his early evening hiking upstream in search of game. To avoid detection by the elders of the Indian village, he stayed a good distance away from the bank for one hour as he headed east, then went back down to the river in the early dusk. He shot a hawk, and roasted it on a fire right where he was, before heading back down the north side of the river in near darkness. Meanwhile, the boys headed back to Wakchumni without so much as a frog.

"You were gone all day, and you couldn't even bring back one squirrel, or rabbit or frog?" Aunt Macha asked the threesome when they returned empty-handed in the late afternoon. "What did you do all day?"

Wabakashiek did not want to answer, for he had disobeyed his father's orders. But Guyape was more forthcoming. Wabakashiek cringed as his younger friend answered: "We helped a man cut up a bunch of trees. Then, somehow, we joined the trees together like this," Guyape said, touching his left hand to his right at a 90-degree angle, just like the fence they had built.

"No, not a bunch of trees, nit-wit!" Wabakashiek screamed. "One tree! And a bunch of big sticks that he had in a tent on circles!"

"Don't call your friend a nit-wit!" Aunt Macha retorted. "You are the nit-wit for saying the sticks were not trees. If they are made of wood, they had to come from trees. And how do you put a tent on circles!"

Tashi, who was nearby sharpening arrowheads, heard the commotion and came up to them. He had seen covered wagons in Mariposa, and knew right away that the boys had made contact with "another" White man.

"Wabakashiek, was this man White? Don't lie to me son!" he yelled.

"Yes Papa, he was White," Wabakashiek said, holding his head in shame. "It was the same one I saw a few months ago, he just set his tent downstream this time."

"You will have to be punished. But Guyape and Sahale will also be! All three of you, go find some switches on the river!" The boys did as they were told, selecting branches from the willow tree near their village. Meanwhile, Tashi told the fathers of Guyape and Sahale what their sons had done. These men gave their sons lashings that stung and left welts.

Tashi was much angrier with Wabakashiek. He waited until the other men were done lashing their sons, then struck Wabakashiek with all three willow branches. The force of impact against Wabakashiek's back was so strong, bits of flesh fell off of his back, leaving welts so deep they bled. It was too much to endure without screaming, so Wabakashiek let out blood-curdling yells which the whole village heard, until finally, Tashi stopped. Wabakashiek ran down to the river to cool his back, and stayed there until dark.

By that time, the rest of the village had eaten their suppers and were gathered around the camp fire for story time. As Wabakashiek approached, Chief Red Hawk led the village in the familiar prayer chant:

> *My words are tied in one*
> *With the great mountains,*
> *With the great rocks,*
> *With the great trees,*
> *In one with my body*
> *And my heart.*
>
> *You all do help me*
> *With supernatural power.*
> *And you, Day!*
> *And you, Night!*
> *All of you see me*
> *One with this world!*

CHAPTER 6

Wabakashiek was in too much pain to sleep well that night. It also was hard for him, because laying his back to the ground was too excruciatingly painful, but laying on his stomach or side all night wasn't comfortable either. Not only was his back sore from the still bloody welts from his father's lashing, his muscles hurt because of all the heavy lifting he had helped Eastman do the day before. The next morning he woke up at dawn, but was hurting too much to do more than lay stomach down on a rock and enjoy the emerging sunlight. Guyape and Sahale meanwhile, were ready for another adventure with the White man.

"We are going up to that White man's tent again today," Guyape told him, out of earshot of the adults and the younger children, who might potentially tattle. "Are you coming with us?"

"No, I don't think so," Wabakashiek responded. "It was fun helping him, but my whole body aches now! And what did we get for it, except for half a squirrel? Was half a squirrel worth all that?"

Guyape and Sahale left without their slightly older companion and headed down to Eastman's tent. When they got there, they told him what had happened the night before. Eastman, understanding just enough to know what they said, frowned.

He realized if he was going to have any help from the people of the Indian village upstream from him, it would only be the three young boys with whom he'd already made contact. And they would not be able to remain safely in their village if they were going to work with him. There was only one thing he could do. He could tell the Justice of the Peace these children were being abused, and take custody of them for himself.

"I guess finishing the fence is going to have to wait," he told the boys. "I'm going to have to take care of some legal matters first. You guys go back and take care of Wabakashiek. I'll be gone for a few days, and hopefully, he will feel better when I get back."

With that, Eastman got up and fed the oxen by scattering a week's worth of grain in front of them. He then saddled up his horse, pointed at the boys and back to their village, and rode off. Guyape and Sahale looked west as he rode off, wondering what they had said to offend him. They also wondered why he left without the oxen, and what would happen to them.

After he had returned from his hawk dinner the night before, Eastman had unyoked these oxen from the wagon. He then cut the 100 feet of rope he'd brought with him into six sections, so that he could tie each ox to a section of the fence. He had hoped with the boys' help, the next day he would have finished the other three sides of the corral, so that the animals wouldn't need restraint. Now, he would have to keep the oxen tied up for quite a while.

Eastman had no idea where California had established its county lines the year before. He knew that in Sonora, he had lived in Tuolumne County. He mistakenly assumed his new camp next to Shehamniu also was, and headed back up to his former home.

Clara, Eliza and John were happy to see their husband and father a mere two and one half weeks after he left home. This was earlier than they had expected. He had told them he would return later in the summer, after harvesting and selling his wheat crop. But in 1851, the harvest alone should have taken nearly two weeks. Also, completely escaping Eastman was the fact he had returned to Sonora on July 3, 1851. This was technically the day before California's first Independence Day, since it had been formally admitted to the United States in September the previous year.

"Papa, I am so happy you are back," Eliza said, running out the door to greet him when she saw her father approaching. "You came for the Fourth of July. Everyone is so excited about that. Did you know that here in California, it is the very first Fourth of July?"

"Is today the Fourth of July? Eastman asked. "I'm so glad I get to spend it with you Eliza, and your mother, and John.

"No, silly Papa. Tomorrow is the Fourth of July!" Eliza said. "We are going to go to a picnic at Judge Creamer's house. We will have fried chicken and apple pie and all kinds of fruit! And we will play games!"

Sonora didn't actually have a courthouse in 1851, so Eastman was surprised to hear Eliza reference Charles Creamer as "Judge Creamer." Then he remembered that Tuolumne County was setting up its own courthouse, and would be holding trials later that month. Creamer had been appointed the new judge by Gov. McConnel before his first trip to the flatlands. Creamer was just the man he needed to talk to about the Indian boys he had left behind, Eastman figured.

"Well that sounds like it will be a lot of fun, Eliza. It will be good to meet Judge Creamer. I suppose he is the same man who was Mr. Creamer the last time I talked to him!"

Yes, Papa," Eliza replied. "He is Mr. Creamer. But now Mama says we are supposed to call him Judge Creamer."

"Ralph, how did you manage to get away for the Fourth of July?" Clara asked, coming outside to see whom Eliza was speaking with.

"Eliza, you run along now," Eastman said. "I have some things I need to discuss with your mother. I'll fill you in later, OK?"

"This sounds serious," Clara said as Eliza went back into the house.

"Let's just sit on our veranda and talk about it a bit," Eastman replied. The two sat on the wooden chairs Eastman had made last year, and he began to tell her about the events of the past few days.

"So, what I'm going to have to do is take these three boys into my own custody," he said. "The two younger ones were telling me the oldest one got beat so bad he could hardly walk! No child should have to endure that!"

"What dreadful savages they are," Clara said. "Still, I feel for their mothers. No mother should ever have to endure losing her child. So many do from death. But those mothers will never know if their boys are dead or alive. They will always be wondering, always be worrying."

"And if they could put it all in the good Lord's hands, those women would know their sons are going to have a better life!" Eastman said. "But I doubt they will be able to do that. You know, the last night I was there, I heard them chanting in their native tongue. It was kind of like the Miwok chants we've heard here, but a little different. All I know is neither one of those chants are anything that would come out of a godly man or woman's mouth!"

"Well, I guess then, God would want us to go down there and help at least three boys to find out how civilized people are supposed to live," Clara said. "So will we be going to the flatlands soon?"

Eastman shook his head. He would have to tell Clara now that once he returned, it would be about a year before he could send for them. Furthermore, without this year's wheat crop, it was going to be a difficult year for all of them.

"No, I'm sorry," Eastman said. "Those savages not only beat their children, they also stole all the wheat from me. This means I cannot leave again until the wheat is harvested next year. You and the children will have to remain up here until then."

"In the meantime, I will talk to Judge Creamer tomorrow about this situation with the boys. Under California law, because of this abuse, I can take custody of them. Since tomorrow is Friday and a holiday, it will probably take until Monday to get it worked out. Then I'll go back down to the flatlands with some officers of the law. Once I get the boys, we will still have to finish building the corral. We got a good start last week, but then I had to head back up here. Once the corral is built, we will have to build the barn and the house. And I won't dare leave next year's wheat crop alone after what happened to this year's!"

"We're just going to have to get by the best we can until next summer," Eastman continued. "I will do OK. But you are probably going to have to do something to help. You have such a beautiful garden, maybe you can sell fruit and vegetables to the miners."

"I'll do my best. Maybe I can even hunt a few animals!" Clara said.

"That's my girl!" Eastman replied. "You are an amazing woman!"

The next day, just as families all over the United States did in 1851, the Eastman family of Sonora, California put on their finest clothes for the holiday. That meant long flouncy gowns and bonnets for Clara and Eliza, knickers and starched white shirts for Eastman and his son John. The material wasn't as ornate as what some families wore on the East Coast, but the clothes were definitely fancier than what the pioneers wore most days.

Judge Creamer, who had made his living as a lawyer prior to starting his service as the first Tuolumne County judge, didn't live in a modest cabin like most of the recent settlers. He had already built a two-story home of white clapboard, and had surrounded it with green grass, hedges and flowering plants. It was located in the rapidly growing "downtown Sonora," area, unlike the Eastman house which was a plain brown single-story cabin near Woods Creek in the Sonora Knolls.

The judge's servants had draped red, white and blue bunting along the railing above his front veranda, making the white house look as festive as any southern plantation. In the front yard, a long table draped in white linen held the food Mrs. Creamer had prepared, as well as that which her guests brought to share. Thus, this table was laden with fried and boiled meats, mashed potatoes, loaves of white bread, bowls of freshly churned butter, fresh and canned fruits and vegetables, lemonade, tea, pies, cakes and cookies.

This celebration, being California's first Independence Day as part of the United States, was a much larger deal than most holidays were in the middle of the 19th century. In other states, most families typically celebrated Independence Day more quietly. Fireworks, community picnics and parades became typical much, much later – more than 100 years later. Christmas also was much less ostentatious than in modern times.

There was one other event, brand new to California at that time, but now commonly part of large summer gatherings. That is the baseball game. Baseball had been invented in Cooperstown, N.Y. in 1839 and was slowly sweeping the nation. It had come to California in 1849 when professional baseball team founder Andrew Cartwright arrived in search of gold. By 1851, it was commonly played when large groups of men could find enough open space to set up a makeshift diamond.

In San Francisco, a group of men had organized as a professional team. However, professional baseball as we know it today was more than 100 years from coming to California as the first two Major League teams didn't relocate to California until 1958. In the 1850s, the San Francisco Knickers got paid by Cartwright, but played amateurs all over the northern part of California. They had even come to Sonora to play men there once. They were elsewhere on July 4, 1851. Judge Creamer had so much property that he was able to create a diamond of home plate and three bases, with one of his hedges serving as a backstop. It was Eastman's first time playing the game, but the rest of the men had organized other pick-up games throughout the spring and summer months at various locations in Sonora.

Meanwhile, as the ladies finished last minute preparations on the food, the children engaged in such games as marbles for boys, hopscotch for girls, hide and seek, tag and three-legged races for both. Most of the teen-aged boys were involved in the baseball game. The teen-aged girls were either helping the younger children with play, helping their mothers in the kitchen or watching their favorite boys on the baseball field.

Once the baseball game was over, everyone gathered around the table. There weren't enough chairs, so the people at Sonora and California's first Independence Day celebration took their portions of this mid-day meal buffet style. Then each family sat down on the sprawling grass lawn of Judge Creamer's estate, some on blankets, others directly on the grass. Once he and Judge Creamer finished eating their food, Mayor Charles Dodge rose and clanged a bell.

"Could I have your attention, please?" Dodge asked the crowd. "Today is a momentous occasion! Today we are celebrating the first Independence Day in the City of Sonora, and in the State of California! Today in Sacramento, our new state capitol, and across the country in Washington, D.C. our friends and countrymen are unfurling a new flag with 31 stars, because California is the 31st state! May that star shine brighter than all the other stars, and may California become known as the finest state in all the Union! Long live California! Hooray!

Everyone joined in hollering "Hooray for California!" as they did all across the country in most of its cities in towns. They did this in Sonora, in Agua Fria, in many other towns that had formed in northern and central California because of the Gold Rush, in Sacramento, in San Francisco, in San Jose, in Los Angeles and in San Diego.

The only places there were not celebrations were on the Indian reservations many of the Native Americans had already been sent to, and in Native American villages like Shehamniu. There, the people neither knew nor cared about California or the United States. And Wabakashiek, Guyape and Sahale had no idea it would be one of the last days they were truly free.

After Dodge's speech, Eastman approached Judge Creamer, and told him about his adventures in the flatlands. He told him about planting the wheat, coming back to "civilization" to work at the port of Stockton for several months, and returning to the farm a few months later to find the wheat crop destroyed. He told them about how three young Indian boys had been very helpful to him his first day back, but had been severely beaten by their fathers. And he surmised that to succeed in his wheat-growing venture, he would need these boys to help him without fear of retaliation.

"Yes, you are right, the Act for the Government and Protection of Indians would allow you to take the boys as your indentured servants," Judge Creamer said. "But there is only one problem. I cannot authorize this. It appears you have gone way south of Big Oak Flat, and that area is in the County of Mariposa. Stay the weekend, Ralph. Enjoy time with your family. Then on Monday, you can ride over to Agua Fria and get the matter taken care of there."

Eastman did exactly that. Saturday, July 5 he spent a relaxing day simply enjoying the company of his family. He did make a trip to the general store to purchase two more bags of wheat and adequate clothing for the three boys. Although there were no Protestant churches in Sonora in 1851, the Eastman family observed the Sabbath on Sunday July, 6 as they always had, by singing hymns and reading scriptures.

The next day, Eastman began heading to Agua Fria. It was a sad day for him, as he was saying good-bye for a year to the family he had in Sonora. Not making him feel any better, he knew soon, he'd have a new "family" of three Native American boys. Although he thought taking the boys from their family was in their best interest as well as his, his heart was still heavy about the violent means by which he would have to accomplish this. Adding to his conflicted feelings, he wouldn't be asking people in Sonora whom he knew to handle the dirty work. He would be asking complete strangers in Agua Fria for this help.

Eastman arrived in Agua Fria the evening of July 7, and camped by a stream there. The next morning, he shaved, put on a clean shirt and looked around the small community of Agua Fria. He quickly located a log cabin where Sheriff James Burney operated the first Mariposa County sheriff's station. Burney then went with Eastman to contact the local judge, Justice of the Peace James Bondurant.

Bondurant supported efforts by the people of Mariposa County to domesticate Native Americans and use them as servants. When Eastman explained to him about the three Indian boys living down in the valley, Bondurant directed Sheriff Burney to send deputies Crippen and Nelson down to the valley to assist Eastman in seizing the boys. The three of them left that morning, and arrived at Shehamniu early the following afternoon.

Tashi was the first to notice the three White men riding on horseback as they approached Shehamniu.

"Do you see that?" he asked Chief Red Hawk. "I knew they wouldn't leave us alone. Let's make sure they know they are not welcome here!

Chief Red Hawk agreed with the plan. He, along with Tashi and Achachak, mounted the horses and rode out to confront the three strangers. The rest of the men waited in the village, ready to fire arrows if the trio fought their way past the chief and his two escorts.

"Why you here?" Chief Red Hawk asked, in English.

"Your village has boys who have been abused by their fathers," said Deputy Crippen. "Those boys will be taken into our custody and turned over to Mr. Eastman here. He will provide for their needs until they reach full adulthood, at which time the boys can choose if they wish to return to this village or continue to live in a more civilized fashion."

Since Chief Red Hawk knew nothing of the Act for the Government and Protection of Indians, the answer to his question made no sense.

"No go!" he told the White men, folding his arms across his chest, then pointing back upstream, signifying his wish the men would head back in that direction.

"Go we must," the deputy told him. With that, Eastman and the deputies pushed past the Native American riders to the edge of Shehamniu. Immediately, arrows flew from the bows from all the other men in the village, and from those of Wabakashiek, Guyape and Sahale. One arrow hit Eastman's horse in the foot. Another critically injured Deputy Crippin's horse, so severely that he fell to the ground.

"There are the three boys I must take," Eastman said when he spotted Wabakashiek, Guyape and Sahale.

He waved to the boys. They put their bows down and waved back. Meanwhile, the adult men were loading arrows that more certainly would have hit one of the White men.
But then the people of Shehamniu heard something new. It was gunfire, from Deputy Nelson's revolver. They also saw the bullet from this gun whiz into the middle of the plaza, where it plopped, shiny, into the ground.

"My weapon is much more powerful than your bows and arrows," Deputy Nelson said. "And I can shoot five more of these bullets without reloading. So, you can either surrender the three boys, or you can all die. Makes no difference to me. I'll be taking Deputy Crippen back to Mariposa either way once we're done. I'd just as soon shoot you all right now so there won't be any more problems, but that's not what's on my orders. If you surrender peacefully, the rest of you can stay right here. And as I understand it, your boys are going just a little ways downstream."

Eastman was now standing by the boys, and motioned for them to follow him. The boys were afraid, but Eastman then whispered to Wabakashiek "Those bullets will hurt your father much more than he can hurt you. You will save his life if you come with me." To further emphasize his point, Eastman pointed his index finger towards Tashi, and said "Pow, pow."

Wabakashiek could see that Eastman was concerned about the deputy who had fired the strange device into the village square. He didn't really want to leave Papa, Aunt Macha or anyone else in Shehamniu. But, he didn't want to be near the two strange White men either. He shook Eastman's hand and said "We go."

With that, the three boys turned to follow Eastman out of the village. Guyape and Sahale didn't understand why they were going, but could see that Wabakashiek was more afraid to stay than to follow Eastman.

"Why are you following him?" Sahale asked.

"We have to!" Wabakashiek replied. "That one deputy has a gun, and if we do not follow Eastman, he will use it on our fathers. Since Eastman is a kind man, it is better we go with him and let our fathers live!"

As they left, Deputy Crippen followed them. Deputy Nelson remained in the center of the village to make sure no one else approached. He glared at the Native Americans in the same way a man might stare down a wild animal, with a mixture of fear and loathing.

"Thank you for cooperating," he told the village men after Eastman, Deputy Crippen and the boys had left. "Your boys will have a better life this way. And, for their sakes, we will make sure your village isn't displaced." He didn't really feel the village should have been spared, nor that he owed the men any gratitude, but gave his guests these platitudes because his job dictated he must.

Neither the three boys nor anyone else in their village realized Eastman wasn't just borrowing the boys for a few hours as he had the week before. This time Eastman would keep them, just as James Savage kept the three young men who worked in his store. Eastman was, in a sense, now the master of the three boys.

Many Native American children were taken from their families and forced to work as slaves for White people in this same manner. Both boys and girls were captured. The girls were legally obligated to stay with their new families until the age of 25 (long past typical marriage age of a White woman in those days), and the boys could legally be kept until they were 30 years old. The White settlers of Gold Rush era California also captured Native American adults by accusing them of crimes, having them arrested and paying "bail" to a judge. Instead of being tried for their alleged crimes, the Native Americans were forced to work for their redeemers for many years.

Eastman, however, was a kind master. In fact, that first day, he required no work of his three new servants. Once they had made the way down to the chopped oak tree, Eastman himself carried up enough wood for that night's fire. He then shot four squirrels, so that he and the boys could enjoy them with slices of the sourdough bread he'd brought back from Sonora.

He then entertained the boys by singing "Crown Him With Many Crowns" and other hymns, all a Capella. Eastman and his family had regularly attended an Episcopalian Church before living in California. Since there were no Protestant churches in Sonora during the years they lived there, they did not regularly attend church once they moved west. Instead they worshipped on Sunday mornings as a single family. Even though it was Thursday, Eastman extended the tradition that day to include his new "family" of Wabakashiek, Guyape and Sahale, whom he called William, Guy and Sam.

Eastman then spread out blankets so he and the boys could sleep by the campfire. Although at first the boys attempted to leave for the familiarity of their village, when Eastman pointed his fingers and imitated the sound of popping bullets, the boys realized that would be their fate if they left that night. They all slept very well that night.

The next morning, Eastman produced shirts, breeches and jeans for the boys and thrust these at them. The boys had no clue what to do with them, but Eastman showed them by pulling his own jeans over the breeches he'd slept in the night before. Eastman had made sure he bought the clothes a larger size than the boys would actually wear, so that they would fit loose and perhaps last for two years.

Eastman then put his own socks and boots on. Because ill-fitting shoes, either tight or loose, could damage a growing boy's foot, and because these boys had gone barefoot all their lives, Eastman had not purchased them footwear. That was fine with them.

He then felt he needed to cut their hair. He walked over to Wabakashiek, whom he called William, and grabbed a lock of his long hair.

"You'll be first William. This won't hurt."

Eastman then raised the scissors.

"Yahhh!" Wabakashiek screamed. "What are you going to do to me?"

Eastman, not being a great barber, and having a none-too-willing first time customer, cut the back of Wabakashiek's hair to collar length, and the front only slightly shorter. Once he finished, Wabakashiek rubbed the back of his neck, which now lay exposed to the sun.

"What have you done?" he screamed.

"I'm sure in time you will appreciate the haircut, William," Eastman said. "Guy you're next, Sam you will go after that." Eastman repeated the process with Guyape and Sahale, who not only screamed but cried.

"Don't worry boys. I'm not going to hit you for crying," Eastman said. "Only savages do that."

Over the next few months, Eastman and the boys finished the corral, then a barn. In the late afternoon, they helped him hunt and prepare game animals, and search for seeds and berries to have with them. They also hunted for seeds and grass for the horse and oxen to eat.

After dark, Eastman lit kerosene lanterns and read his Bible to the boys. He used what few words of Miwok he knew, and lots of physical gestures, to explain what he was saying. He did the same in the fields, communicating what he needed the boys to do. It wasn't long before the boys had a limited understanding of the English language. Over time, this would grow to a fluency adequate for them to communicate well with White people.

This family of one father and three "sons" also had to take on the domestic responsibilities normally given to women. Eastman taught them how to fry meat. None of them knew how to cook bread, but with some trial and error the boys figured out how to create acorn mush. The dish didn't agree much with Eastman's palate, but he ate it just so he could add some starch to his diet. In time, he grew as fond of acorn mush as the boys were.

The boys also helped Eastman build the first floor of his house, which they finished in mid-November 1851. It was large enough to provide dining and sleeping quarters for one man now, a family of four soon. It didn't have room for Indians though.

The boys weren't happy when Eastman told them they could not join him. They had become quite accustomed to sleeping in the open air next to his tent. After Eastman went into the cabin, leaving the boys with only the fire to keep warm on a cool November evening, they discussed this change in events.

"We ought to just go back to Shehamniu, where at least we had a roof over our head!" Guyape said.

"But Eastman might have bullets," Sahale said. "Bullets are dangerous."

"Maybe if we stay here, Eastman will let us build a wiki-up for ourselves tomorrow," Wabakashiek said. "Let's just go to sleep."

This was not easy, because by morning a light rain was falling. But, having spent their entire lives with nothing more than a wiki-up to take cover, the boys weren't terribly fazed. They were still asleep when the sun came over the mountains the following morning. The red hawk's screeching woke them up, but Eastman was there a short time later. He woke them up, grabbed the wet blankets and took them to the barn.

"You boys should have slept in here! Didn't you know it started raining during the night?" he asked them.

"A barn is for animals," Wabakashiek said.

"And for Redskins," Eastman responded. "You are William Redskin, and your friends are Guy Redskin and Sam Redskin. The barn we built is more solid, and warmer than anything you have ever slept in before. The rain will be even worse tonight than it was last night. To me, given the choice of the barn and the cold ground, I would take the barn any day."

"Wiki-ups are for Redskins," Wabakashiek argued.

"Then build a wiki-up" Eastman said. "If it's going to be that much better than a barn, build a wiki-up."

Before doing anything else that morning, the boys went to the river. They broke a bunch of branches from the willow trees, and shaped them into wiki-ups just as their forefathers had done for centuries before. Each boy built his own wiki-up.

Eastman also approved their request all four of them go into the mountains to hunt animals, for meat and because their skins would provide the same warmth and cushioning they were accustomed to at home. He insisted, however, they head north into the hills he was familiar with, instead of east past Shehamniu. This was on the upper reaches of the Merced River, where the Native American boys' families had traded with Miwoks from time to time. These were the Miwoks who were now living on reservations because of the treaty signed earlier in 1851.

CHAPTER 7

In early Spring 1852, they planted a new wheat crop. This one was twice as large as the one before it, because Eastman had picked up two more bags of wheat seed during his second trip to Sonora in 1851, as well as the two he'd obtained the first time. Since Eastman had built his house, barn and corral a mile downstream, the new wheat field didn't reach quite down to the old one.

Since they were still relying on rainfall and a high groundwater table to grow wheat, they didn't have to spend all spring and summer irrigating it as a modern farmer would. They just had to make sure the horse and the oxen had enough to eat, even if it meant scraping the dry wild grass. In late July 1852, they harvested the wheat. Eastman himself operated the grain cradle he'd brought down the year before.

He had the boys follow behind him, tying the wheat into shocks, which somewhat resembled, but were shorter than, the wiki-ups in which the boys and the people of Shehamniu lived. This was tedious work, but in the early 1850s there were no horse-drawn mechanical reapers that could speed the process. It took them two weeks just to harvest the wheat.

They left the shocks in the field to dry. A week later, the boys helped Eastman carry them into his barn. There, Eastman took a linen cloth and laid it in the middle of the barn. They placed the wheat, one shock at a time on the floor. Eastman then showed them how to use a threshing flail to separate the wheat heads from the stalks, and how to winnow away the straw. Taking turns, they had all the wheat threshed within another week.

Eastman raked the straw to the side of the barn near the horse's indoor corral. Although he would be taking the animals with him on his upcoming journey, they would need the straw in the fall months, when the dried grass grew sparser. It was also likely that Clara would be able to cover a portion of the straw with cloth, thus creating a mattress for them to sleep on in their new cabin.

The horse, who now enjoyed half of the corral to herself, could come from her side into a second, smaller pen inside the barn. She would be fed there. The oxen's side of the corral extended to one of the barn's uncovered windows. They could be fed the straw when a person pitched it through the window to them.

Eastman also had brought a plow on the wagon when he came back from Sonora the first time. This meant, unlike in early 1851, he wouldn't have to cut a tree down to scrape the ground to the condition he wanted it. He simply hooked the horse to the plow, and scraped both the new field and the field that had been abandoned a year earlier to the condition he wanted it.

The people of Shehamniu noticed Eastman as he plowed the old field. But, he had asked the boys not to come with him. Since the Shehamniu residents didn't see their sons, and presumed them to be dead anyhow, they let Eastman plow his field in peace.

When Eastman was finished plowing both fields, it was time for him to return to Stockton to sell his wheat, and then to Sonora to pick up his family. This would mean he would be gone for two and a half weeks, and then his family would begin their new life on the farm. He decided to wait until morning to explain all this to the boys.

"I'm going to have to leave again for a while," he told them. "I will be taking the animals with me. You guys will stay here. There's nothing much to do, so just enjoy summer like all children do. The only thing is, you get to do it without any adults telling you how."

Eastman needed the boys to help him move the six oxen out of the corral and over to the wagon, where he yoked them, pair by pair, to the front. He then tied his horse to the side of the wagon. As they secured the animals, Wabakashiek commented on the situation.

"It's been a long time since you left," Wabakashiek said. "You miss the mountains?"

"I miss my family," Eastman replied.

"I miss mine too," Wabakashiek told him.

"I know. But you are better off with me," Eastman replied. "We are going to grow more wheat each year. By the time you are a grown man, there may even be opportunities for you to grow your own wheat, make your own money and live in a house, not a hut."

"I like living in a wiki-up," Wabakashiek said.

"But some day, you will see a house is better," Eastman replied. This was true, because when the three boys grew up, they would all live in houses. In fact, it would turn out that Eastman would help Wabakashiek build his.

"Have a good trip, Eastman," Wabakashiek said.

"That's Mr. Eastman!" he replied, even though all three boys had never included "Mister" when they addressed him by name. "You're in charge, William. Make sure Guy and Sam behave themselves."

"Ok, I will," Wabakashiek replied. "Goodbye!"

After Guyape and Sahale had said their good-byes as well, Eastman went to the wagon's buckboard. "Wagon's ho!" he told the oxen, cracking two of them with his whip. That was their signal to begin moving downstream for the long trip to Stockton. As he left, he noticed the red hawk flying above the boys' wiki-ups. When Eastman had left, the boys pondered what they should do with their complete freedom.

"Let's go hunting!" Sahale said.

"That's a great idea," Guyape and Wabakashiek both agreed.

"Let's make some new bows and arrows before we go!" Wabakashiek said. "That way we can get big animals if we see them."

The boys spent their first day of freedom bending three large willow branches into bows, stretching the bark of another willow branch to complete them. The next day, they left early in the morning, each taking their bows and a dozen straight sticks to the foothills, where they had a better chance of finding sharp rocks they could use to carve other sharp rocks into arrowheads, as they had been doing for years before. The boys went all the way to the plateaus that had been, up until the year before, the dividing ground between their village's grounds and those of the Chauchila and Ahwaneechee tribes.

In keeping with tradition, and in fear of what had happened to their elders, the boys went no further. They didn't need to though because by the end of that first day, each one of them had a deer. There was no reason for them to go back downstream, so they remained on the plateau for 14 days, enjoying several more deer, as well as squirrels and birds.

When they came back, Eastman still had not returned. They didn't want him to be mad, so they decided to stay on the farm. They made "fishing baskets," which is how the Chaushilha and all Yokuts historically caught fish. They also made snares to trap coyote and foxes, using the same methods their forefathers had for centuries.

When Eastman returned to Sonora on August 10, 1852 it had been more than 13 months since he'd seen his family. When he arrived this time Clara, Elizabeth and John all ran out to greet him.

"Ralph! You made it home! We are so glad!"

"Papa, you're back! I was getting worried!" Eliza said. John, still too young to express himself in complete sentences simply said "Papa! Papa!" over and over again.

"Eliza you don't need to worry your pretty little head. Papa always wanted to come back and get you! Now, guess what! When I leave again soon, you and Mama and John are coming with me!"

Eliza, now 8 years old, was surprised.

"You mean we're going to leave Sonora? But I like it here! All my friends are here!"

"You will like it on the farm too," Eastman reassured her. "And maybe you will want to be friends with the Indian girls!"

"I don't know Papa. Aren't they savages?" Eliza asked.

"Not the girls!" Eastman replied.

"Ok then, I'll go," Eliza said.

"That's my girl," Eastman replied. "Brave and ready for an adventure. How about it Clara? Are you ready for one too?"

"I guess I have to be," she said. But tell me, will I have anything in common with the women there?"

"I don't honestly know, seeing as how the only time I met any of them was when I was taking three of their sons away from them," Eastman answered. "I guess you would have in common with them that you love your children, just like they do. And that you will love three of their children, just like they did."

"I hope they don't hate me for that, Ralph" Clara replied.

In reality, it would be several years before the Eastman family met anyone other than Wabakashiek, Guyape and Sahale. As they made the trip from Sonora to their farm, they realized there would be too much risk to the family if they attempted contact with the Natives. They would have to quietly live their lives on the farm, and wait for circumstances to change before they interacted with others outside their family of seven.

Eastman had already sold the grain in Stockton. He also had stopped there to visit his brother, Richard Eastman and his family. Richard, who had come to California in the same wagon train as his brother, sought gold to begin with. Finding some, he established a store on the Stockton waterfront, and was also instrumental in bringing the city's first Episcopalian Church to that city.

In Sonora, Ralph Eastman purchased two dairy cows for the trip down to the farm, and lots of fruit and vegetable seeds. This would allow Clara to milk the cows and churn butter. Along with her homemade sourdough bread, the fruits and vegetables she could grow in her garden, plus whatever animals he could hunt, would provide them all the food they would need. The combination of Clara's cooking and gardening talents, plus his ability to hunt would ensure they ate better than anyone had in the family all the previous 13 months, as Clara and the children did not have meat to eat most days Eastman was gone, and he did not have fresh produce or bread most of the days.

After a big breakfast at the Sonora Inn, the Eastman family began their trek down to their farm to begin their new life on Aug. 11, 1852. They arrived 10 days later. Greeting them were Wabakashiek, Sahale and Guyape, who were wearing the traditional Native American male garb – almost nothing. Eliza and Carolyn both shrieked when they saw the boys, and John began crying.

"No need to be scared," Eastman said. "These boys are William, Guy and Sam. Boys, these people are my wife Clara, my daughter Eliza and my son John."

"Very nice to meet you, mam," Wabakashiek said to Clara. "My name is really Wabakashiek, but you can call me William. These boys are Guyape and Sahale, but Mr. Eastman likes to call them Guy and Sam."

"Those were your old names!" Eastman said, emphasizing the word "old." "My family will call you by your Christian names. This will make your life go better."

Sunday came a few days later. Since there was no church to go to, Eastman built a campfire, and asked his family, including the three adopted Native American boys, to join him. He led his family in the singing of his favorite hymn, "Crown Him With Many Crowns." He then shared a basic gospel message of how God sent Jesus, his only begotten son, to Earth to redeem those who believe from their sins.

Wabakashiek remembered the creation story his tribal elders had said by many campfires before. He began reciting what he could remember: "Long ago, there was a great flood."

"Hey, we believe there was a great flood a long time ago too!" Eliza interrupted. "You mean to tell me you guys already knew about Noah's ark before my Daddy told you anything?"

"I don't even know what an ark is, but I'll keep telling you what happened here, OK?" Wabakashiek said. Without waiting for Eliza's answer, he continued his version of the creation story. "One day an eagle and a crow flew out of the sky, searching for a place to land."

"You're right, first it was a crow, but then it was a dove!" Eliza interrupted, not knowing how anyone could get the story of Noah's Ark so very wrong.

"If it was a dove, I'm eating it!" Wabakashiek said. "But OK, if you really like doves just because they're doves, I guess it could have been a dove. Anyways, both of them were out there flying over the flood, looking for a place to land. There were some small fish swimming about in the water, so both Eagle, I mean Dove, and Crow, were swooping down and eating the fish."

"It doesn't say that!" Eliza whined.

"It does in my story, which is the one we have been telling here for many generations," Wabakashiek said. "So my story is the true one. The birds both flew to great heights to survey the land," he continued. And, actually it does have to be an eagle, not a dove. Because, the eagle can fly better than a crow, and that's what this one did. But neither he nor the crow could find land."

"Not for 40 days anyhow," Eliza said. "Then the crow ran away, and the dove came back."

"I don't think the dove went anywhere," Wabakashiek said. "But the crow stayed with the eagle. Maybe it was 40 days they kept looking, I don't know. Let's say it was. After 40 days, they saw a duck swimming in the water. Like they had been doing all along, the duck was catching fish in the water. It caught more fish than the crow or the eagle did. It also brought mud up from the bottom of the sea.

"Eagle and Crow wondered. Could Duck bring up enough mud to fill in the sea? We need to tell Duck that's what we need! So they worked out a deal where they would catch fish for Duck, only he needed to go down to the bottom and get mud to trade for the fish.

"Duck put the mud on a tree stump that rose up above the water. As he did this, Eagle and Crow spread their wings to move all the mud to the side of the stump they were standing on, Eagle to one side and Crow to the other. It took a long time, but eventually both birds had big piles of mud on either side. They started putting fish on their mud piles, which made Duck work even harder to get even more mud. One day – maybe 40 days after all that – the three birds realized, and said in bird talk, "We are making a whole new world!

 "Eventually, the water started lowering a little bit on the sides of their world," Wabakashiek continued. They all agreed 'Surely, the flood is coming to an end!' So they went out further to look. Eagle went really far away, and did not come back for a long, long time. It was night when he came back. But in the meantime, Crow kept putting more mud on his pile. So when Eagle got back, he was mad, because there was twice as much mud on Crow's pile. He didn't think that was fair. I never thought about this before, but I guess sometimes, some birds and some people too, think they should have more than everyone else."

"But anyways, he asked Crow "Is this your idea of sharing the world equally?" That just led to fighting between Crow and Eagle all the next day. But the day after that, they started making their new world again. Eagle decided, to make up for while he was gone, he would catch twice as many fish for Duck. Duck gave him twice as much mud as he did Crow, so before long, Eagle's pile of mud was way bigger than Crow's. Eagle saw it and liked it, but Crow never even noticed.

"Finally, they looked through the water and saw land. They hoped that soon they would have a better place to stand than just the stump separating the two mud piles. But there still was a long time before they did. Because, before the first water came all the way down, there was more thunder, and more lightening, and more rain! So, Eagle and Crow each dug holes in their mud piles so they would stay dry. Duck liked the rain, so he just swam around on top. But the rain fell all night, and it washed away the world Eagle and Crow had built. But the three birds talked in bird talk, and decided that had just been to clean things up. They would start over and build their whole new world again. But Eagle still caught twice as many fish as Crow did, so Duck gave him twice as much mud. This time, Eagle built his pile so high it became those mountains," Wabakashiek said, pointing east. "And Crow built so high, it became those mountains."

The mountains these days are known as the Sierra Nevada and the Coast Range. But to Wabakashiek, they were the Eagle Mountains and the Crow Mountains.

"That story doesn't even make sense," Eliza said. "Before we lived in Sonora, a few years ago we went over those big mountains. There were some even bigger ones before them. Then there was lots and lots of land over the other mountains. It took us six months to get all the way from where we were to Sonora. And Papa says there is a lot more world past there, past where we live now too. There are things called oceans, he says. How could three birds make all that! They didn't make all that! God did! And then God did make a flood, because people were bad. He wiped out all the people, except for a man named Noah, and his family. Noah kept all the animals on an ark, and everyone except the crow and a dove stayed on the ark until the water dried up. But the dove, he did find an olive tree before that. So I guess maybe there were trees. And I don't know how these mountains got there."

"I suppose either one of these stories could be true," Eastman said. "It's one of those things we will have to ask God when we get there. William, Sam and Guy, maybe some people will insist things happened the way Eliza said. But I don't know for sure. What I do know is there is a God, and he does hear what we have to say. So, now we must pray."

Eastman and his family folded their hands in prayer. The boys stood silently, but when Eastman finished his prayer, they chanted the Yokut Prayer, which just like Eastman's, offered thanks to God. As they prayed, the red hawk silently circled overhead.

CHAPTER 8

Life for Wabakashiek, Sahale, and Guyupe didn't change too much after Clara, Eliza and John joined them on the farm. Just as they had been doing for more than a year before that time, they spent a good portion of their day helping Eastman take care of his animals and his wheat crop, and they spent a good deal of the night learning reading and writing, math and how government worked for the state of California and for the country of the United States.

On Sundays, they would sing one hymn, after which Eastman would read a passage of Scripture. He started with Genesis and how it explains the world's creation, and also moved onto the verses that formed the Noah's Ark story Eliza had interjected that first week. Other days he told them about other Old Testament patriarchs, like Isaac, Joseph and Abraham. Around Christmas, he started telling them about Jesus.

Eastman thought every civilized man should know the Bible stories. But, he wasn't really sure if they were more true than what the Indians around him believed. So, he had no objections to the boys telling their own stories, and he allowed them to close their Sunday worship by praying the Yokut prayer.

Each summer, Eastman took one boy with him when he went to Stockton to sell grain. He left the other two with his family, with the understanding they would protect them in case of attack by the nearby Indian village. Guyape and Sahale were confident they could do this. Wabakashiek, on the other hand, remembered the attack his people and the other two tribes' warriors had made on the store when he was a small boy, and doubted much two young Native American boys, two small children and a woman could fend off his village. But, lest Eastman think he was a savage for having participated in that raid on the store, he said nothing about it to any of the others.

For Clara and her children, life was much harder than it had ever been before. There were no other children for them to play with in the neighborhood, because Clara was afraid to walk upstream to where the Indian village was. The only Indian boys either Eliza or John played with were the ones they called William, Guy and Sam, and then only when the boys weren't busy helping Papa with the animals and fields, or with their lessons. Since Eliza knew more, academically, than the boys did, she sat in on the lessons her Papa taught, as did John.

Eastman built not just a second story on the cabin, but a completely new home after selling the 1853 wheat harvest at a particularly good price, $2.19 a bushel. With a fantastic profit and three boys' help, he erected a two-story white clapboard home with a parlor, living room and kitchen downstairs and three bedrooms upstairs. That gave Emily and John their own rooms. The older boys still weren't welcome in the home, but that was fine with them. They still liked living in a wiki-up.

Five years later, things changed even more. That was when Eastman met Henry Miller. The meeting took place on the San Joaquin River, where all of them were camping out. Eastman was on his way to Stockton with Wabakashiek and the 1858 wheat crop. Miller was with his crew boss Robert Turner and eight other men, escorting the Miller and Lux Company's first 400 herd of cattle to their new home in the San Joaquin Valley.

Miller was no stranger to these animals in 1858, because he and business partner Charles Lux had been operating a butcher shop in San Francisco since 1850. But now, they wanted to diversify and raise cattle for the growing California population. They were hoping to find men like Ralph Eastman, whom they could hire to grow cattle feed. The numbers of cattle they planned to bring to the San Joaquin Valley would not be satisfied by the wild grass growing there, so their diet would have to be supplemented with barley, oat and wheat seeds.

Miller and Lux would end up owning 1.4 million acres of land, primarily on the "Westside" area of the San Joaquin Valley, nearer to the Coast Range than the Sierra Nevada. In 1858, they had already headquartered their cattle operation north of the present-day city of Los Banos. Spanish-American settlers had started coming into Los Banos in the early 1840s, and by 1858 there were plenty of Whites as well.

"Woah, Eastman," that's a lot of cattle," Wabakashiek said when they approached Miller's camp along the San Joaquin River. "Why does he need that many?"

"I don't know," Eastman said. "Let's ask."

"Howdy boys!" said Robert Turner, crew boss. "Where you headed?

"We are taking this wheat to Stockton, sir," Eastman replied. "I grew it on a field downstream from here."

"Is that right!" Turner said. "See all these cattle? We are taking them down the San Joaquin River just a little ways further. We will need to partner with grain growers. You have any experience growing anything besides wheat?"

"I have only grown wheat, sir," Eastman said. "I have been doing that since 1851. Except for the first year, when my crop got stolen by a bunch of Redskins, I've done quite well. My family has a nice home by one of the rivers that feeds into this big one."

"And now you travel with a Redskin!" Turner said, eyeing 18-year-old Wabakashiek carefully. "Are you sure this man won't steal your wheat?"

"He has lived with me since he was a young boy," Eastman said. "He is well-schooled now in the ways of civilized people. If it weren't for the fact he still insists on living in a tee-pee, I would forget he is a Redskin. Oh, and the fact that his name is William Louis Redskin, or at least it would be if he had a birth certificate."

Wabakashiek said nothing. He knew it was best the other White men come to know him as William, not his birth name. He didn't know what a certificate was, but he did know if he had one, it would have said "Wabakashiek." Nor did he know what a tee-pee was.

"You have any other help on your farm?" Turner asked.

"There are two other Redskin boys who live with William," Eastman replied. "I don't know if they really are blood brothers, but they come from the same village as William, and I call them Guy Redskin and Sam Redskin."

"Maybe you could find some more from the village?" Turner asked.

"I doubt it," Eastman said. "William's father was very much opposed to the boys visiting with me when I first arrived. He beat William severely, and also made sure Guy and Sam were punished. I contacted the law and got custody of the boys after that. We haven't had any contact with the rest of the Indian village since then."

"Well, I hope you can find some more, but three workers will do for now. Because I think you can help us. We are purchasing a great deal of land in California, including 100,000 acres in Los Banos. These 400 head of cattle are just a start. They are going to eat the grass growing there, but then what if that runs out? And after we slaughter these, what will the cattle we bring in after them eat? It is best we form alliances with men who are already established in the area as grain growers. Are you in?"

"It sounds intriguing," Eastman said.

"Ok, let me have you meet the boss," Turner said.

In 1858, Henry Miller was only 30 years old, 13 years younger than Eastman. But he was already a wealthy man, so had come down from San Francisco riding inside one of the covered wagons his entourage was pulling. His black suit and starched white shirt, therefore, looked almost as clean as the day they had left. Dressed finely, he had an air of superiority over his ranch hands and over Eastman.

"Hello, I'm Ralph Eastman," Eastman said, extending his hand.

"Glad to meet you, I'm Henry Miller," Miller said. "I hear you'd like to work with us."

"Yes sir!" Eastman said.

"Very good! I tell you what. Don't worry about that wheat crop you have with you now. We will buy it from you for double what you got last year. Instead, take back these bags of grain and plant them."

The next morning, Miller paid Eastman $4,380 for his wheat crop, which was twice what he had made the year before. He then sold Eastman eight bags of grain for $40, which would be enough for him to plant 160 acres for his 1859 crop. That was twice the acreage he had planted from 1852 to 1858.

Miller was acquiring vast land holdings through land grants and by financing the purchase and resale of property by other men. In other cases, discouraged ranchers were selling out to him, and going to work for him. This included most of the nine men, including Robert Turner, who accompanied him the day he met Ralph Eastman. But, he could tell from the quality of wheat Eastman had carried with him this was no ordinary farmer. Eastman would instead be a good grower.

Thus, from then on Eastman grew grain for Miller & Lux, an arrangement that lasted nearly 30 years, until Eastman's death in 1887. In the first few years, Eastman expanded his operations from 80 acres to 1,200 acres.

Eastman also bought the latest in farm technology, such as a bigger plow for planting, a horse-drawn combine harvester and a horse-drawn thresher. This required him to buy more horses, but his crew could harvest and thresh as much wheat in a single day with the new equipment as they previously had in a week. However, since Eastman's acreage grew from 160 acres in 1858 to 1,200 by 1861, he had to find new sources of labor.

The first few years, it turned out he didn't have to look too far. When Eastman had kidnapped Wabakashiek, Guyape and Sahale, the people of Shehamniu – with memories of the Mariposa War fresh in their mind – had developed an even deeper distrust of White men. But, since Eastman had left them alone after that, by 1858 their feelings about him had changed. One day, events happened to bring him even closer to the people of Shehamniu.

With no other children to play with, the friendships Eliza Eastman developed with William, Guy and Sam Redskin grew stronger and stronger. She found William Redskin the most interesting of the three. He also had taken on a protective role, making sure she not fall prey to the practical jokes Guyape and Sahale tried to pull on her.

One summer evening, not long after Eastman and Wabakashiek had returned from meeting Henry Miller, the foursome engaged in their favorite game "Bear." This was a Yokut game, similar to "tag" boys and girls often play now. One child is the "bear," and chases after the others. When he or she catches another child, that one becomes the bear.

When the Native American boys played it, Eliza being younger, weaker and encumbered by long skirts, rarely was able to tag one of her friends. Wabakashiek felt sorry for her, so he would sometimes let her catch him. Besides, he loved being the bear. He would run around growling, terrorizing her and annoying Guyape and Sahale.

Because Eliza had played "hide and seek" with other children before she moved to the farm, she had a habit of hiding in the barn when the boys played Bear. The boys knew this, and when they were younger children, often found places to hide from the Bear as well. They also knew they could look for her in the barn if they were Bear.

In 1858, she was 14 years old, and was growing tired of silly games. The younger boys, even though they were 16 years old at the time, were just as rambunctious as they had always been, and now were dealing with raging hormones as well. So, after Wabakashiek had tagged Guyape as the Bear, he and Sahale ran for the barn, knowing they had easy prey there in the form of Eliza. Wabakashiek, who at 18 was getting tired of Bear as well, remained outside to hear Eastman's strategy on planting the grain Henry Miller had given him.

Suddenly, they heard Eliza shrieking. When they ran into the barn, they saw her laying on the floor and Guyape standing over her. He had just kissed her, and was attempting to place his hand up her skirt to brush it against her crotch when she screamed. Hormones had overtaken Guyape in a way he could not handle, and he temporarily lost control of the urges battling within him. Sahale was his biggest cheerleader.

Wabakashiek, on the other hand, could not bear to hear Eliza shriek. He grabbed Guyape and punched him in the face. In Yokutsan, he screamed "Don't you ever touch that girl like that again! If you do, the beating my father gave me before we came to live with Eastman will seem like a tickling!"

"Don't you dare touch my daughter like that you savage!" Eastman said. "I ought to give you a beating right now!"

Guyape heard "beating" in both languages, and came to his senses. "I understand sir. I am sorry. I didn't mean to hurt your daughter."

"Don't let it happen again," Eastman said. "And go to your hut! You too Sam! I can't stand to look at either one of you right now!"

Wabakashiek, meanwhile, helped Eliza to her feet.

"Are you hurt?" he asked. "If you are, I will beat Guyape up."

"That's all right. I am a tough girl. But tell him, I do not want to play Bear with him ever again!"

"I don't like Bear either," Wabakashiek said. "It is such a stupid game. We used to play a lot of other games when we were little. The elders joined in. But they were dangerous games. In one, we had to throw spears through rolling hoops, whoever got the most spears through the hoops won. In another game, we hit a ball with sticks, and whoever got their ball to the end of the field the most times won."

"We have some better games than Bear too," Eliza said. "We have Battledore and Shuttlecock. I play it with my mother. We hit the shuttlecocks, those are a piece of wood with some feathers attached with the battledores, those are bigger pieces of wood with strings across them. I don't even know who wins, Mother and I just hit them around."

"I would love to play that game with you someday, Eliza" Wabakashiek said.

"William, I am not sure I like that idea," Eastman said, having sent the other two boys away. "But I do respect you for treating Eliza like a gentleman should. I think she has had enough for tonight, so I will let you go deal with Guy and Sam however you want to go deal with them. Tomorrow, if you would like to play our games with her, after breakfast we can send your friends off. Eliza and I will show you our games, and you can play them with her. I would appreciate though, if you also include John. He doesn't have any friends his age, and now that he is 10 years old, he should have some other boys to play with. But you are the only boy I can trust right now. Guy and Sam have always played too rough with him."

"Sure, John can play too," Wabakashiek replied. "I like John. I wish he could have met the little boys in my village, he would have friends like Guyape and Sahale are to me. They are good boys."

"Well, maybe someday we will go up to the village and see if any boys would like to come down here," Eastman said. "John is almost as old as you were when I first met you, and I think he's about the same age Guy and Sam were. So, I am surprised none of them have gone on an adventure like you three did."

CHAPTER 9

The next morning, Eastman was still angry with Guyape and Sahale for what had happened in the barn. "Guy and Sam, you boys go upstream today. Find some meat for us to eat. Go back to your village. I don't care. Just get out of here!"

Guyape and Sahale were puzzled why Eastman would want them to go back to their village after all these years. They weren't sure if the villagers would receive them, especially since they were dressed in the clothes of a White man. Still, they made a plan to check the old village out.

In 1858, the people of Shehamniu were still living much as they had in the past. Following Yokut tradition, once Wabakashiek, Guyape and Sahale were kidnapped and presumed dead, their names were not brought up again. So, it was a shocking and fearful moment when the two dark-skinned but White-dressed men showed up that summer morning.

"Men, prepare to attack!" Tashi, who had replaced Red Hawk as the chief a few years before, sounded out this warning. But Guyape and Sahale raised up their hands and shouted, in Yokutsan, "We come in peace!"

"Who are you?" Tashi asked.

"Guyape and Sahale," Guyape said. "The White man did not kill us, nor did he kill Wabakashiek when he took us many years ago. We have been living on his farm all these years, and it has grown much larger. He has a daughter, and she has grown up to be a beautiful young woman. But I guess Eastman thinks we should have Chaushilha women for ourselves. Last night I touched Eliza, his daughter. He is furious with both Sahale and me now, and told us to go back to the village!"

"You shouldn't touch women without their father's permission," Tashi said. "But what's this about Wabakashiek? He is still alive? How come the White man didn't let him come back?"

"Wabakashiek acts more like a White man than we do nowadays," Guyape explained. "He treats Eliza like a little sister instead of like a girl he wants to get to know better. I guess that makes him more like a son to Eastman."

"Yet surely he wants one of his own women?" Tashi said. "Or does he plan on finding a White woman?"

"I don't know," Guyape said. "But I guess we are still Chaushilhas. So maybe we need to stay here!"

"You will have to pull your load if you do," Tashi said. "You can worry about finding women later. Right now, we need to go upstream and find some meat. It is getting harder and harder. Mariposa, where the Chauchila lived, is now exploding with White people. The White people have also built many homes near Okhumhurst. They are cutting down the trees in Okhumhurst and Mariposa and making lumber out of them. They are employing a lot of the Ahwaneechee and Chauchila off the reservation, and some of the men from our village who were a little bit older than you two as well. Maybe you boys will want to go up there and find work?"

"Let's go up there and hunt," Sahale said. "If they have pretty women, and nice fathers, we will stay."

Sahale and Guyape did indeed stay in Mariposa when the hunting party went there a few days later. Tashi had negotiated a peace treaty with the deputies of that community. This means they were able to trade baskets made by their women for food and tools, and they were free to come and go as they pleased. This also allowed some of the young men from Shehamniu to leave the village and work at the lumber plant.

When Tashi introduced Sahale and Guyape to Lawrence Holmes, a lumber plant superintendent in Mariposa, Holmes was glad to see the strong, young men. A fire had recently burned down much of Mariposa, and it would need a lot of lumber to replace those buildings. This meant he needed more lumberjacks. When these two willingly put on the plaid shirts, 501 jeans and sturdy boots offered them, he was even more pleased.

"It looks like these boys will fit right in, Tashi. Thank you for bringing them to me," Holmes said.

"They are better off with White men," Tashi said. "They have been living with one for the last seven years anyhow. They might as well stay White. They do not belong in Shehamniu anymore."

Tashi started to explain to Sahale and Guyape the plan, but the boys had understood every word. They were surprised Tashi had learned English.

"Where did you learn to speak English?" Guyape asked.

"Every man has to speak English nowadays," Tashi said. "It is the only way to survive. Our village will probably die soon. The young men have all found work here in Mariposa, or down in Fresno Flats, which is what they call Okhumhurst now. The young women go with them, they find things to do up here in the mountains too. The girls I could have offered you that are still in Shehamniu, they don't even have breasts yet. Better you find girls here!"

As his companions scurried away from Eastman, Wabakashiek had watched them. He saw how they ran up the hill towards Shehamniu, and wondered if he should follow. But Eastman assured him he still was very much welcome to stay at the ranch.

"I don't want to show those two what we do here," Eastman said. "If I brought the games and toys out for them, they probably would just walk right in some evening and steal the games after they assaulted Eliza. I cannot trust them! But I would like to show you a game called 'Game of Graces.' It does sound like the hoops and spears game you were talking about last night, and I think you might enjoy it. I'll be right back."

Eastman returned from inside his home with two 7" hoops, to which four faded red ribbons were attached. He also had four sticks that appeared to be about a foot and a half long, carved smooth and even from lumber. He then beckoned for Eliza to join him, and they took turns using the sticks to lift and spin one of the hoop through the air. The object of the game was that they would catch the spinning hoops on the sticks, but neither Eliza nor her father were very good at that.

"You take over," Eastman said to Wabakashiek after a few minutes, handing him two of the sticks. "I'll play the other hoop with John."

When they were by themselves, Wabakashiek and his two friends had entertained each other with their own version of "Spears and Hoops." Two boys would roll hoops they had made from willow limbs between them, and the third would attempt to throw three-foot long sticks through the moving hoop. This was similar to the game they had played with men and other boys in their village, but in those days they had to be careful. All the men were throwing sticks, so if you got in front of one of your opponents, you might end up getting hit by a stick. They played this game to develop accuracy when hunting with spears. For Wabakashiek, it had already paid off. He had one of the best aims of anyone in or near Shehamniu. So, when Eliza sent the little ribbon-tied hoop through the air, Wabakashiek had no trouble aiming a stick right through the hoop. The only problem was, unlike in Spears and Hoops, one is not supposed to let go of the stick when playing Game of Graces.

"That was really good for the first time playing it," Eliza said. "But why did you let go?"

"Wild animals don't come to you, so what good is letting the hoop do so?" Wabakashiek asked.

"What does Game of Graces have to do with wild animals?" Eliza responded.

"I don't know what this Game of Graces is, but you play Spears and Hoops by throwing the sticks at the moving hoops," Wabakashiek said. "But I guess that's too hard for a girl. Let's see if you can catch it instead."

Wabakashiek sent the hoop spinning and flying towards Eliza, much faster than her parents had ever done so. When it came over to her, it was spinning out of control, so she screamed and ducked.

"That's not how you catch a hoop!" Wabakashiek said. "Send it back over to me, and I'll see if I can catch it your way."

Eliza gently tossed the hoop with her sticks, so lightly it barely stayed in the air. Wabakashiek lunged forward so he could catch it with his. He was successful, but as he steadied his arms, he fell headfirst right into Eliza's skirt. Then he stood up, pulling her closer to him in an embrace.

Then he kissed her. Eliza, who had dreamed this would happen, closed her eyes and let William's tongue roll around in her mouth. Gently, she let her tongue do the same in his.

"I'm sorry, Eliza. I should not have done that," Wabakashiek said when they were done kissing. "Your father would not approve."

"Never mind my father, William," Eliza replied. "I am a young woman now. He cannot keep me a little girl forever. But there are no men my age around here, except for you and your friends. Am I supposed to grow up to never know the love of a man? It cannot be! I love you!"

"You are still too young, Eliza," Wabakashiek said. "But you are beautiful. I will just have to keep my emotions in check. It probably is better, also that I find a young woman from the village to marry. You and I are not the same kind of people. I will talk to Guy and Sam when they come back, and perhaps all three of us will return to our village soon. For now, I am going to go back to my wiki-up."

Eliza walked over to where her father and brother were playing their Game of Graces.

"Where did William go?" John asked.

"He went back to his hut. I think he got mad because I told him you weren't supposed to throw the sticks," Eliza said.

"Silly William," John said, going right back to trying to run his stick through the hoop Eastman sent his way.

"Papa, if it is all right with you, I will go inside and fry some chicken, and some mashed potatoes. Then I will take him a box lunch, the chicken, the potatoes and some fresh fruit. We can have a picnic down on the river! I think he will really like that!"

"I don't think you and he should have a picnic by yourselves," Eastman replied. "No telling what would happen. He is a gentleman, but he is still a Redskin. So, we will all go with you, and we will all five have a picnic by the river."

Wabakashiek had hoped he would find Guyape and Sahale at the wiki-ups, but figured they had made plans to go somewhere else. He figured they might even be heading several days away from the ranch after the threat of beating both he and Eastman had given Guyape. He gathered some rocks and began sharpening them into arrowheads, in case he too would need to go hunting for his next meal.

A few hours later, the four Eastmans showed up at Wabakashiek's wiki-up with chicken, mashed potatoes, strawberries, tomatoes and some green beans that Clara had canned a few days before. They also had five plates, five knives, five forks and five cloth napkins. Clara and Eliza sat the plates down in a row, then with the spoons and pair of tongs they had also brought down, put the food on each plate. When they were done, Eastman grabbed one plate for himself, one for Wabakashiek, and handed the second plate to him.

"Here William. We made you a special lunch. Please enjoy it," Eastman said. "Then please come back up the house, and I will show you even more of the toys and games Eliza and John enjoy playing."

Wabakashiek did not want Eastman to be angry with him, so he ate the meal prepared for him quietly. Eliza kept staring at him, but he dared not speak to her. He could not let anyone in her family, nor her, know how much he really wanted to just take her into his arms again.

After lunch, he followed the Eastmans back up to their home. To his surprise, Eastman invited him in. There were things in this home he had never seen before, all of which Eastman had hauled down from Sonora and slipped into the house when the boys weren't looking. This included a cast-iron stove and oven, a large mahogany dining table with four upholstered chairs, and an ornately carved, slightly upholstered davenport with two matching chairs. All of the upholstery on the six chairs and the davenport was black, chosen so that it would not show the dirt of a farmhouse. But, there wasn't that much dirt, because this farmhouse had a floor of smooth wooden planks, covered with a rug Clara had braided from scraps of brightly colored calico. This was similar to the bolts of fabric Wabakashiek had seen in the store many years before, but he had not seen rugs, furniture or cast-iron appliances before.

"Have a seat," Eastman said, motioning to the davenport. Next to one of the chairs, backed up to a perpendicular wall, were a piano and a piano bench. Eliza sat on the bench, while John went with Eastman up the stairs. Clara seated herself on the chair on the opposite side of the couch.

Eastman and John returned from upstairs with John's wagon full of blocks, and set them down at Wabakashiek's feet. "Look William," John said. "We can build a house with these. Or a barn. Or maybe even a big hotel like they have in Sonora!"

Wabakashiek laughed. "I don't think those pieces of wood would be good for building much more than a fire pit!"

"Oh yes they would," said John. "Let me show you!" He began stacking the blocks so they formed what looked like a small house. "See, it's a house."

"You used almost half your blocks just to build a house that isn't even as tall as you are," Wabakashiek said. "How are you going to make it big enough for people? When I was your age, I didn't need silly blocks. I could take a bunch of sticks, bend them up over my head and build a wiki-up! And I did! My wiki-up has lasted me for the last six years! How long is your house going to last? Six seconds!" When he finished speaking, he knocked John's blocks down.

"Okay, I guess blocks wouldn't be that exciting for a White boy William's age either," Eastman said. "But we do have other things in here you might like. We have that Battledore and Shuttlecock game Eliza likes so much. We have card games we can teach you. We have nine pins. We have a ring toss game. And we have two big hoops that Eliza and John like to roll around."

"Big hoops sound interesting. I have a big hoop down at my wiki-up too, I made it myself. Let me see yours," Wabakashiek said.

John went back upstairs, got both the hoops and gave one to Wabakashiek. He then motioned for Wabakshiek to follow him outside, which he did. Eliza, Clara and Eastman also followed them.

John rolled his hoop, but Wabakashiek did not do likewise. Instead, he picked up a stick from the Eastman's lawn, and threw it right through John's hoop. This was actually harder to do than catching the smaller hoop on the two sticks.

"Wow, you are so amazing," Eliza said. "How can you throw a stick through a hoop that is rolling that fast?"

"Years of practice!" Wabakashiek said. "Now, how about you and John roll the hoops, and I'll throw my sticks through them? Then, I will show you both how I can throw sharpened sticks through flying birds too!"

Eliza and her mother kept a henhouse full of chickens in the barn, so they were no strangers to animal butchery. They lopped the heads off of live chickens, plucked their feathers and hacked them into chicken parts on a weekly basis, except for those weeks when Papa had been able to kill the deer, fox or coyotes that wandered onto their property. Or was it William who had killed them?

"I've never seen anyone kill a bird that was flying in the air," she said. "If you do, I will pluck that bird for you, and we will have fried birds for dinner even though we had fried chicken already for lunch."

At that moment, a red hawk flew over the lawn. Wabakashiek picked up his stick, which wasn't even sharp, and aimed it towards the hawk as powerfully as he could. He hit the target, and with such force, the hawk fluttered down to the ground, dead. Wabakashiek had completely forgotten the tradition in Shehamniu to not kill hawks.

"There you go, Eliza," Wabakashiek said. "Fried hawk for dinner! Yum, yum!"

"I can't believe you killed such a beautiful bird," Eliza said. "But it will be a good dinner, and I will gladly prepare that dinner for you, William Redskin."

Eliza plucked the hawk, then cut it into pieces so she could fry them. But first, she took the big pot out of the cupboard and began boiling potatoes for the second time that day. She also picked five ears of corn, which she shucked and boiled. Then she fried the hawk pieces in lard on the cast-iron frying pan they kept on top of the cast-iron stove. At 14, she had already cooked dinner for her family more than a few times, because mother was busy tending the garden, washing and mending clothes, and otherwise keeping a house as clean as it could be on a farm surrounded for miles and miles by dirt.

Meanwhile, Wabakashiek continued to play hoops, then marbles with John and his father. He also showed them how to play "shinney," which both father and son recognized as similar to hockey. It was almost sundown when Liza walked out to the yard and told them dinner was ready.

After dinner, Eastman again invited Wabakashiek to sit on the davenport. This time, Liza sat facing the piano, and began to play from a hymnal. Wabakashiek knew the words to many of the songs from the Sunday morning worship, so he joined the Eastmans in singing along. It was very dark when Eastman headed back down to his wiki-up But, more so than ever, he felt like he was part of the Eastman family.

CHAPTER 10

After returning from Mariposa, Tashi went by himself downstream. If his son Wabakashiek was alive, he wanted to see him again. He wanted to tell him he forgave what happened. He knew now it would have been inevitable for Wabakashiek to have encountered White men somewhere, and to have left Shehamniu for the easier life the White men seemed to have. So, it did not matter now that Wabakashiek had done so years earlier than most of the young men in his village.

When Tashi approached the village, he noticed the three wiki-ups first. He went right up to them, calling his son's name. This, as well as the mournful cry of a female hawk, woke Wabakashiek up.

"Guyape, Sahale, are you guys back?" he said. Guyape and Sahale both had the voices of men, but this one sounded different. Yet familiar.

"Wabakashiek, it's Papa," Tashi said.

"Papa! My papa now is Eastman that lives in the big house!" Wabakashiek replied.

"No, I am your Papa," Tashi said. "And I know where Guyape and Sahale are."

With that, Wabakashiek came out of his wiki-up. He'd been sleeping with his Native American style breeches on, and didn't need to get further dressed for a member of his own village, much less his own father.

"You know where Guyape and Sahale are?" he asked. "They took it seriously when Eastman told them to go back to where they came from?"

"Yes, I guess there was a misunderstanding about the girl Eliza," Tashi said. "I am sure neither one of them had intended any harm. They are good boys. But I do know they are safe. We went hunting, all the way up to Mariposa. They went with us, and found work at a lumber yard there. So, they will be staying up there from now on, because there is no future for young men in Shehamniu. I should know, as I am the chief of Shehamniu now."

"Congratulations, Papa," Wabakashiek said.

"Are you doing all right here? Is the White man treating you properly?" Tashi asked.

"Yes Papa, he is treating me very well," Wabakashiek said. "He calls me William Redskin, but that's OK. A few days ago, he even let me into his house!"

"Is that right?" Tashi said. "I guess you really are one of the family now!"

"Yes, I suppose so," Wabakashiek said. "But you will always be my family too. And Aunt Macha, and Uncle Achachak and my cousins. How are they?"

"They are all doing well," Tashi said. "We have to go a lot farther for the food these days, usually all the way up to Mariposa or what they now call Fresno Flats, it was Okhumhurst, several times a year. As far as I'm concerned, those places are ours, whatever they call them. But there are a lot of White people in both places, all over the place up there. They don't see it that way. But, we work things out. At least they haven't come down and stolen any more of our children!"

"Well, I don't have to go very far for food. I just have to go up to the house, and all my meals are taken care of. I do help Eastman with hunting sometimes. But I'm sure they have some oatmeal and fruit ready for breakfast right now. Would you like to go up there with me and see?"

"Sure," Tashi said.

"OK, there's just one thing," Wabakashiek said. "I'm going to put my White man clothes on, and you need to grab some from over there, those belonged to Sahale and Guyape. Eliza and her mother Clara get really upset when they see me in nothing but a breech cloth. And after what Guyape did the other day, it might be even worse now!"

When Wabakashiek and his father were fully dressed, they walked up to Eastman's house. Clara was outside gathering eggs from the henhouse, as that was part of their plan for breakfast. They at first thought the two men coming up to them were Wabakashiek and one of the other boys, and were quite startled when they noticed the man with Wabakashiek was much older. Then it was Wabakashiek's turn to be startled.

"Howdy mam," Tashi said to Clara, in perfect English. "I am Chief Tashi from the village on the other side of this hill, and I am Wabakashiek's father. He says you are taking good care of him, but since you had two other boys leave your farm the other day, I wanted to be sure for myself."

"That's understandable," Clara said, as puzzled as Wabakashiek was that an old Native American man she had never met before could speak English. She knew there was a village upstream from them, and she knew Wabakashiek was the name William used in that village. Still, he had never said anything about his father being the village chief, nor had he mentioned anyone his village knowing how to speak English.

"When did you learn to speak English, Papa?" Wabakashiek asked, in Yokutsan.

"It is necessary to speak English now to survive," Tashi said, in English. "We don't just hunt for wild animals in the mountains anymore. We take our women's baskets up there, and we trade them for food, guns, tools and other things they sell in their stores."

"You have civilized dealings with the people in Mariposa?" Clara asked. "Then you can have civilized dealings with us too. Please stay for breakfast, Chief Tashi."

"I would be glad to," Tashi replied.

Tashi was familiar with eggs, because he had purchased chickens from the stores in the mountains, and now had a flock of egg layers. However, he was not familiar with the "sunny side up" way of preparing them, nor with using silver utensils. The Chaushilhas had cooked their eggs scrambled on hot rocks, then used acorn bread to pick up and hold the eggs.

Clara and Eliza were serving their sunny side up eggs with slices of sourdough, spread with jam. Tashi wasn't even sure what the purple substance on the strange, thick bread was. Nor did he immediately recognize the white disks with orangeish-yellow centers as eggs. But, before Eastman had begun to say grace, he picked up the bread and tried to pull the egg onto it with his other hand.

"Papa, that is not how to eat in a White man's house," Wabakashiek said. "Plus, they ask their god to bless their food before they eat it. Let Eastman say the blessing, and then I will quietly show you how to eat the White way."

"I don't need you to show me," Tashi said. "I will wait for him to bless the food, because it is right to honor your gods. But, I have been eating my food the way I eat my food for more than 40 years now. It may be different food these days, but I still have two good hands with which to eat!"

"Don't worry then," Eastman said, remembering enough of the Miwok language to sort of understand what the other two men were saying in Yokutsan. "Just enjoy your breakfast. After breakfast, I have an idea I hope you will like."

Wabakashiek and Tashi were curious about this idea, but ate their food without saying anything more. After Eliza and Clara took the breakfast dishes into the house, and John was dismissed to do his chores, Eastman asked the two Native American men to remain.

"I was given a very, very good price for the wheat fields this year," Eastman began. "So, I can plant even more next year. I will also begin farming barley and oats, which will be for the cattle rancher who bought my wheat this year. But I would like to know two things. First, may I plant closer to your village without having you tear the field up? Second, I will need more than three men to help me with that many fields. So are there other young men who can help me besides William and the two other boys who have been living with me?"

"You will not have the help of Guyape and Sahale anymore," Tashi said. "They have found work for another White man, in Mariposa. When they told me what happened here a few days ago, I figured that was for the best. When Wabakashiek told me his version of what happened, I became even more sure. Guyape's behavior was unacceptable, and no woman should be subjected to that."

"You are a reasonable man," Eastman said. "If Guy and Sam cannot work here, are there others who can?"

"I could. So could five or six other men in my village," Tashi said. "But they are not young men. All the men who are only a little bit older than Wabakashiek have left the village, the same way Guyape and Sahale left us. They find White men in the mountains to work for, and the White men offer a better life. I hope you are giving Wabakashiek a better life too, but there are not many people here. The women his age, they have also all left. Where will he find a wife?"

"I worry the same for my children," Eastman said. "They are still too young. But it will not be long. I do take William or one of the other boys to Stockton with me once a year to sell the grain. Still, we do not see many women on that trip. However, I was hoping William would stay with me for a long time. If he does, I may have to give him Eliza in marriage."

"We can worry about that later," Tashi said. "Let's talk about the men who can help. Except for me, they are all married with families. I help support the large family of Achachak, because he has 10 children, and his wife Macha was sister to Wabakashiek's mother. Wabakashiek was my only child, but I guess he can take care of himself now. Or let you take care of him.

"But my other men, and myself, we cannot come to live with you on this farm. We will have to come and work, then go back home to our families at the end of the day. That is the only way it can work."

"That will work for me too. Would you like to smoke on it?" Eastman said. He went into the house and brought back two pipes and a bag of tobacco. He put a pinch in each pipe, then lit one and handed it to Tashi, who accepted. Tashi had smoked pipes with men in Mariposa and Fresno Flats, so this wasn't a new experience.

"Peace," Tashi said.

"Peace," Eastman said.

Wabakashiek sat by them. He had seen Eastman smoke pipes before, but this was the first time he knew of his own father doing so. He did not equate the more colorful clay instruments, which we might call "peace pipes" as the same as the smaller wooden pipes his father smoked with Eastman. Wabakashiek watched, taking in the sweet aroma of the tobacco. Although it smelled different, it took him back to times when, as a young child, Tashi and other men would smoke native herbs with men visiting from the other Yokut and Miwok tribes.

"You want one too?" Eastman asked.

"Sure! I have never smoked a pipe, but I would like to try," Wabakashiek said.

Eastman grabbed yet another pipe, as he had eight on his 12-pipe pipe holder. He filled it with tobacco, lit it and handed it to Wabakashiek. But when Wabakashiek inhaled, it burned his throat and he began to cough.

"I guess you and the White man don't have peace yet," Tashi said. "Better leave pipe smoking to grown men."

"Ok, I will, Papa," Tashi said. "It was very good seeing you, and I hope we will get to work soon. But for now, I am going to go jump in the river."

"No, don't leave," Eastman said. "I would like to have your papa's help as soon as possible. Maybe you can go with him to the village to see if the other men will help."

"He doesn't need to come with me," Tashi said. "If I tell my men we need to go help the White man, they will come with me and help you. That is the way things get done in our village. Let Wabakashiek stay here and help you get things done the way you have before."

"All right then. I only have one plow right now, so I will let William stay here and plow under the three fields of stubble I have right now. In the meantime, I will go to Stockton and get two more plows. That way, I can have 400 acres of grain instead of 120, and 20 head of cattle instead of eight. William will finish plowing the first 120 acres before I get back, and he typically has gone hunting somewhere during that time when he wasn't the boy who went with me, which he was this year. Perhaps he would like to go hunting with the men of your village this year?"

"That would be fine," Tashi said. "William, we will see you in a few days, when you finish plowing the 120 acres."

"I have an idea too," Clara said. She had finished washing the breakfast dishes, and was headed back out to the henhouse to feed the chickens, but liked what she overheard the men saying.

"I think your children should receive an education," she said. "I taught school before I married Ralph, back in our former home, St. Louis, MO. I have home-schooled Eliza and John ever since we moved here, although Eliza did attend a regular school for two years when we were in Sonora. Perhaps I could also teach the Indian village children how to read and write English, and how to do counting and money?"

"That would probably be easier than them having to learn English when they grow up," Tashi said. "And maybe you would like to teach our women too. I don't feel right just sending boys to learn from a lady. And if I send the girls, they will be smarter than their mothers. I don't think that would be right either."

"I would be happy to teach your women," Clara said. "I am tired of being the only woman around here."

Wabakashiek finished plowing the first field in two days. On that second day Eastman hitched oxen up to the wagon and headed for Stockton, where he would purchase two plows, another combine and enough grain to plant 280 acres more. With a covered wagon, it was slow travel, so he would not return to the farm until 21 days later.

In the meantime, Wabakashiek escorted Clara, Eliza and John to the village of Shehamniu. Once there, Tashi and Wabakashiek introduced them to the rest of the village people. Unlike the hostilities when Eastman had come into the village years before, the people of Shehamniu were gracious and friendly to their new White visitors.

To them, Wabakashiek had come back from the dead. This meant his return was a special occasion, and had to be celebrated accordingly. So, Macha decided to slaughter one of the steers her men had purchased in Fresno Flats that year. A steer would provide enough meat for the entire village, and the men could easily get more.

Clara and Eliza watched as Macha killed and skinned the steer, then helped her cut it into pieces. Macha did not speak English, and Clara and Eliza spoke no Yokutsan or Miwok language, so communication was only by smiles and gestures.

Macha then seasoned the beef with herbs she had gathered. This fascinated Clara and Eliza, who previously prepared beef by lightly shaking canisters of salt and black pepper onto the meat. They had no idea other seasonings were growing right underneath them.

Once the meat was seasoned, Macha's way to cook it was to place it on the hot rocks she always had going on her camp fire. This also was a new method for the White settlers, who had either previously fried the meat on their stovetop, or baked it in the cast iron wood-fired oven. Macha's way took several more hours than the other women's cooking methods, but the end result was a juicy, tender beef.

By mid-afternoon, it was ready. Macha served the meat with fry bread, and with potatoes and tomatoes. These things were new to the Chaushilha diet since Wabakashiek had last been in Shehamniu, but they were very familiar to him over the last six years.

"No acorn mush, Macha?" he asked, smiling.

"This is better than acorn mush," Macha said. "Eat it up."

The next day, Clara asked Wabakashiek to again take her to Shehamniu, and to explain to his people there her plan for teaching them. The people of Shehamniu were receptive to this plan, especially since Chief Tashi told them it would help them to survive.

So, Clara began by teaching every woman and every child there how to write and say the English alphabet. Once they had their letters mastered, she taught them the English words for the things they used every day. She also taught them how to count, add, subtract and handle American money.

Wabakshiek helped Clara until Eastman came back. Then, there was much work to do. The new variety of wheat Eastman had purchased, both the smaller amount in July, and the larger amount on his recent trip, would be planted in fall rather than spring. This allowed the plants to grow strong underground in the coldest winter months, which in the San Joaquin Valley hover around 40 degrees all day and night. When this wheat sprouted in January, it grew much stronger than the spring wheat Eastman had planted in the past. The name of this wheat was Sonoran, named for the city the Eastmans had lived in for a few years when they first came to California. However, Sonoran wheat did much better on the valley floor than in Sonora, where due to a high elevation temperatures are much colder in the winter time.

For the next few years, the people of Shehamniu lived, for the most part, in harmony with the Eastmans. Although many Chaushilhas continued to live in wiki-ups and worship their ancient religion, they adapted much of the "American" food into their diet, and helped the Eastmans to become fans of their ways of seasoning and cooking it. At planting and harvest seasons, Eastman hired as many men and boys from Shehamniu as he could, and paid them with grain, horses and cattle.

Clara developed close friendships with many of the Chaushilha women. Even though their cultures were quite different, she enjoyed hearing from the older women the stories about how their adult children and grandchildren were getting along. And she enjoyed helping them give advice to the younger women about how to deal with their children. Her friendships were just as good, if not better, than what she'd had with women in Sonora.

One day, she and Macha talked about events that had happened since the day Wabakashiek first met Eastman back in 1851. Macha recalled all the men, even all boys older than Wabakashiek, were in the mountains that day fighting a bloody war, which apparently had started the year before when the men broke into a store.

"I think if it had been the women who made the first contact with you White people, we would have worked things out more peacefully," she said. "We would not have had to steal things, kill or kidnap anyone. We would have just talked to each other, made friends, and worked everything out."

"I agree," Clara replied. "But when do the men ever ask our opinions?" Macha agreed.

John also developed friendships with the Chauishilha boys and girls who were close to his age. At 10, he was more interested in the boys than the girls. Like all of the Chaushilha men before them, John learned with these youngest ones how to hunt with bows and arrows, how to paddle rafts and how to build wiki-ups from willow branches. When hunting in the mountains was necessary, both he and Wabakashiek joined the other males in the village on the expeditions. He became known to all of them as Injun John. And while John and everyone in his family called him William, Wabakashiek was known and called by his birth name to everyone with "red" skin.

CHAPTER 11

The only people who had any problem at all with this arrangement were Wabakashiek and Eliza. Being teenagers, they could not deny the sexual attraction they felt for each other. But, 19th Century morality caused them both to feel uncertain a romantic relationship with each other was appropriate. Had Eastman never gone down to the San Joaquin Valley to farm, Wabakashiek might have found himself a wife from another village than Shehamniu. Eliza probably would have found one of the younger men of Sonora to her liking, or might have traveled on her own to Stockton or even San Francisco to meet her perfect mate. But in Shehamniu and on Eastman's farm, there weren't others suitable for them, only each other.

That first kiss they had shared the morning Guyape and Sahale were sent away became the first of many. There also had been caresses of their fully-clothed bodies. By acts of strong willpower they had not given into the temptations they felt to remove these items of clothing. This was especially hard for Wabakashiek as a man, but he was a strong-willed man, and one determined to be a gentleman.

Most of the time, when he met other White men when traveling with Eastman, they made it clear they found "William's" manners surprising, given his dark Native American complexion. Wabaskiek often wondered why they thought the color of his skin would have any bearing on how he treated people. But this misconception made him all the more determined to behave as a gentleman, especially around Eastman himself. That meant not touching Eastman's daughter inappropriately.

But Eliza wasn't without biological urges. As she matured into womanhood, these grew even stronger than when she was 14. Thus, in 1861, when she was 17 years old, she defied her parents' long-standing orders to stay away from William's wiki-up and slipped down there one night, shortly after Clara and John had gone to bed. As had been the case for several years, her father took one of the village men to Stockton with him instead of William. It was during the time they were away she visited William's wiki-up.

Wabakashiek wasn't really in bed though. He had habitually taken late evening swims in the river, especially in the summer months. This allowed him to go to bed less stinky, less sweaty and less hot than he would if he let a day of hard work stay on his body while he slept. Since he had always been alone, he did what he always did. He went to and from the river without even his Native American breechcloth covering him. Thus, he was stark naked when he saw Eliza standing by his wiki-up that night.

"Eliza, what are you doing down here!" he yelled. "You know better than to come down to my wiki-up at night! A man needs his privacy!"

Eliza had never seen a naked man before, not even John or her father. White people of the 19th century had a modesty that prevented them from showing their most private parts to anyone but a husband or wife. Children and siblings were not afforded any more leeway than a complete stranger when it came to that.

Thus, she was taken aback by Wabakashiek's manhood. Because the river water was cold, Wabakashiek's penis had already started to harden. When he saw her in the moonlight, it went completely erect.

Feeling embarrassed, Wabashiek put his hand onto his penis to cover himself. But this made him want Eliza's hand there even more. Jeans would be impossibly uncomfortable, he figured, so hopefully she would not mind if he put the Native American breechcloth and nothing else on.

This had frightened Eliza when she first met William nearly a decade earlier. But today, she found herself strangely drawn to how William looked in his skimpy outfit. The creamy white cloth almost glowed next to his ruddy brown skin. The cloth also accentuated his firm muscles. And, that bulge beneath it, which was the manhood he was so quick to cover, fascinated Eliza more than anything else.

Wabakashiek also couldn't fight what he was feeling. Eliza wore "bloomers," which were loose flowing pants coming just below her knees. She tucked a collared shirt into these. Thus, her woman-sized breasts and her tight hips were not hidden, just covered. The corset Eliza wore made both the bust and the hips more prominent.

Wabakashiek couldn't help himself. He stepped over to Eliza, kissed her, and placed both of his hands on her bottom. She responded by grabbing his shoulders and pressing her bosom next to his naked chest. Wabakashiek could not keep his hand from sliding down the waistband of Eliza's bloomers, across her pubic mound, and down to her vagina, which he then gently pressed his fingertip into. Coming up, the finger brushed against her clitoris, and she let out a soft moan.

Wabakashiek untied her corset and loosened the drawstring of her bloomers. Then he slipped off his own breech cloth, so that he was naked again.

"I love you, Eliza" he said. "But I respect you. So I will only go further with this if you are ready."

"I love you, and I want you to keep doing what you were doing," Eliza said. "But I am scared. Mama tells me that when you kiss a boy, if you have already become a woman, there are some other things that could happen, and those things will make a baby. But she says people should only do those things when they are married. I definitely do not want to tell Papa I am having a baby, when I am not married. But on the other hand, I do want to have a whole bunch of babies someday. How will that happen if the only man I know is you?"

"Well, then maybe we should get married," Wabakashiek said. "I will talk to your father about that when he returns from Stockton. I will talk to my own father tomorrow. Good-night Eliza Eastman. If you stay here any longer, I am pretty sure 'other things' are going to happen. I am not sure what is necessary to make a baby, but it might be what I am thinking about doing to you."

Eliza then left, but Wabakashiek dreamed of the "other things" that were on his mind when he went to bed. It wasn't long before his semen poured out of his penis, giving his mind and body the relief it needed. He slept restfully the rest of the night, not even noticing the screech of the hawk the next morning.

Eliza, on the other hand, went to bed feeling tense all over and congested in her pelvic region. Rubbing her hand on her privates brought some relief. The thought of pushing her finger into the hole between her legs, a hole she didn't even know the word for, terrified her. She wouldn't even go as deep in, barely a fingertip deep, that William had penetrated already. She woke the next morning feeling she had hardly closed her eyes.

Wabakashiek woke up the next morning with a conundrum. If he went up the hill to join the Eastmans for breakfast, he would see Eliza. He knew he wouldn't look at her the same as he had before. But if he didn't go up there, they would become suspicious and come looking for him. What would he tell them as to why he wouldn't join them? He decided he really wanted acorn mush for breakfast more than toast and eggs, and headed over the hill to Shehamniu.

"Wabakashiek, what brings you here this early?" Macha asked.

"I have a funny feeling in my stomach and thought some of your acorn mush would be the best thing for it," Wabakashiek replied, laughing a little.

"A funny feeling? They didn't make you sick with rich White food over there did they?" Macha asked.

"No, not like that. Their food isn't that rich anyhow. Most of the time anyhow," Wabakashiek said. "Hey Aunt Macha, are you in love with Achachak?"

"Of course I am, Wabakashiek," Macha replied. "How else would we get 10 kids?"

"So love does have something to do with that?" Wabakashiek said.

"Of course!" she replied "Didn't your father tell you that when you were little? And why do you care now?"

"Because I think I am in love with Eliza," Wabakashiek said. "But I don't know if we should be."

"Well, that was bound to happen, with you being raised with only the one girl around," Macha said. "I wish you had grown up here, before all the girls suitable for you were married off to men 10 years older than they are. The only girl left here in Shehamniu that's even close to your age is my daughter Aloette, and she's only 12. Plus, she's your cousin!"

"So, it is natural for a man to fall in love with a girl, even if she is not like him?" Wabakashiek said.

"It is the things about a person that makes him different from you that makes it all that more special," Macha said. "But, I do agree. Eliza is very different from all of us. So we should probably talk to your father and see what he thinks before you go any farther, or decide to tell Mr. Eastman you love his daughter."

Tashi frowned when Macha relayed the conversation she'd had with Wabakashiek to him.

"Wabakashiek, you are living dangerously!" he said. "I told you when you were a boy, White men should not be trusted. Eastman, he has proven himself to be a little different than most White men. But, if you take his daughter as your wife, he may think he owns you. Are you sure that is what you want?"

"I have lived with him for almost 10 years now," Wabakashiek said. "He treats me like family. If I marry his daughter I will be his family."

"And I think he will be okay with it then," Tashi said. "When I first spoke with him a few years ago, we talked about how there were not suitable mates for either one of you. He said, maybe he was joking then, he might have to give you Eliza for your wife. He's going to have to think seriously about that now, because Eliza hasn't seen a White man other than him since she was a little girl!"

"Well, he's seeing other White men himself right now," Wabakashiek said. "He took one of your men with him this time. I wonder if he would ever take Eliza?"

"Hauling wheat is not a job for a woman," Tashi said. "Their job is to take care of their home and their children. Clara has never gone with him either, so far as I know. Why would they even want to?"

"Then I must be the man who will give Eliza what she wants. She can come take care of my wiki-up for me, and I will give her children," Wabakashiek said. "I will tell her father this as soon as he returns."

"And I will stay with you on the farm," Tashi said. "It is hard for a young man to be productive when his thoughts are occupied by a girl. I will make sure you do what you are supposed to do."

Wabakashiek and Tashi immediately left for the farm. Eastman, because he was getting a high price for most of his grain from Henry Miller, had been expanding the farm by a few hundred acres each year. This time around, he intended to plant 1,200 acres – 10 times as much as just four years ago.

This was also the year Eastman intended to expand his operations to the other side of the river, so Wabakashiek would need to plow 400 acres on that side. It was no problem getting himself across the river. Wabakashiek and the others from Shehamniu had been using their rafts to cross back and forth since long before there were wheat fields.

But taking a plow to the other side wouldn't be as easy. When he put the plow on the raft, it started to sink. In those days, before anyone had started diverting water out of the river to irrigate their crops, it created a much wider and deeper channel than now. Even in summer, the river was waist deep to a tall man. A plow falling into the river would have been disastrous.

Wabakashiek quickly pulled the plow back to the banks. "How does that fool Eastman think I'm going to get this big heavy plow over there!" he cried out to his father. Tashi came up with the better idea.

"Son, White men like to put nails in everything," he said. "What if we built a raft so big it could span all the way across the river, and then we nailed it into the ground? Then, it will not fall into the river when we put the plow on it."

It took a lot of sticks to build the bridge raft, about three times as many as one that floats on the river. As Chaushilhas had always done, they lashed the logs together with tule grass. But this big raft had to be constructed by lashing three lengths of branches end on end. This resulted in a raft that wasn't as sturdy at its joints as Wabakashiek and Tashi wanted it to be. The men decided they would brace the joints by nailing larger branches to the underside, and they would also nail them to the end for better balance.

This set the bridge about three inches off the ground, so they would need longer nails than this to nail the bridge to the ground. But in 1861, nails didn't come off a factory assembly line in uniform sizes like they do today. Blacksmiths of that era cut them from iron bars to the size their customers needed.

There were no blacksmiths in Shehamniu, of course. So Tashi and Wabakashiek headed up to Mariposa, trading a basket for 20 six-inch long nails. They planned to nail 10 to each side of their new river-spanning raft. Because they left in mid-afternoon, after spending the earlier part of the day constructing their bridge, it was an overnight trip to the mountains. They also spent part of their time hunting, and did not return to Shehamniu until almost sundown the next afternoon.

Meanwhile, on that first day, Eliza had a conversation with her mother.

"Mother, how did you and Father decide you should get married?" she asked.

"Father is five years older than me, but we went to school together," Clara replied. "He used to give me rides on his horse from school back to our farms, which were right next to each other. They weren't nearly as far from our city, St. Louis, as this place is from anything. So we saw lots of other children every day, at school, at church, and when we went into town for shopping. But, even though he was much older than I, he was the most fun boy to play with. Then we started courting when I was about your age. It just seemed like I would never want to be with another man besides him. So, when he asked me to marry him, I said yes. We got married when I was 18. One year older than you are now."

"I suppose I will be much older than 18 when I get married," Eliza said. "I only know one man who is close to my age, and I am not sure he is the one I should be with forever."

"You mean William?" Clara asked. "Yes, I am sure he is not the right man for you. Although he is a very nice man, he is still an Indian, a savage. It would not be proper for a girl like you to marry an Indian!"

"But then, who will Eliza marry?" Clara thought to herself. She hugged her daughter tightly.

"I will speak to your father about sending you to college," she said. "Uncle Richard told your father there is a seminary for girls in Benicia, and that is close to San Francisco. You will be well-versed in Christian values if you attend there. It will also give you the experience of city life that you need, and I am sure you will meet young men there who would be suitable husbands for you."

Eastman returned from Stockton about an hour before Tashi and Wabakashiek got back from Mariposa. Since the unfinished bridge was down by Wabakashiek's wiki-up, Eastman did not see it. He was pleased, however, that Wabakashiek had already cleared what looked like 800 acres of the fields in which they would plant new grain.

"Looks like William has done a good job clearing the fields on this side. Do you know if he made it to the other side?" he asked Clara.

"I haven't really paid attention to what he was doing out in the fields. The strange thing though, is he hasn't even been up here in two days. Not even for breakfast, lunch or dinner!"

"You haven't seen him in two days?" Eastman said. "I suppose he went hunting. I'll go down and look for him."

"Ralph, before you do, there is something I would like to tell you," Clara said. "Yesterday morning I had a strange conversation with Eliza. She asked me how we decided to get married. I realized she is the same age as I was when we started courting.

"She also pointed out to me she does not know any suitable men. It wasn't like when we were growing up and there were all kinds of other children to play with. She only has John and William. She can't marry her little brother, and she certainly can't marry an Indian savage! I think we should send her to that school for Christian women in Benicia. That would give her exposure to the finer things in life, and perhaps there she would meet a suitable man."

"Wait a second, this is too much to take in. I just got back from Stockton, Clara!" Eastman said. "But I will think and pray about this, and I will give you a decision in the morning. In the meantime, I must find William to discuss plowing the other 400 acres."

Eastman walked down to the river. Since Wabakashiek and his father had not yet returned from Mariposa, they were not there. But their new bridge was.

"That is one amazing raft!" Eastman thought to himself. "It looks as long as the river is wide. I wonder what they're going to do with it, and if it will even float. Maybe they are back in their village. I'll go see."

When he arrived in Shehamniu, Macha came out to greet him. "What do you think of Wabakashiek and Eliza's news?" she asked.

"What news is that?" Eastman replied.

"You mean they didn't tell you?" she said, surprised her nephew and Eliza had kept this exciting news from Eastman. "They are in love. They wish to be married!"

"I haven't even seen William since I got back from Stockton, which was less than a half-hour ago," Eastman said. "But, Clara did tell me something interesting. They had discussed the lack of suitable men for her to marry. Clara thought it would be best to send her to boarding school, so that she might meet men who are like her."

"So Wabakashiek isn't good enough for her, huh?" Macha replied in a huff. "You can't even call him Wabakashiek, so I guess not!

"William, or Wabakashiek if you prefer, is a good man, I didn't mean it that way," Eastman replied. "It's just that___"

"It's just that we are Redskins!" Macha interrupted. "And the Redskins aren't good enough for you, are they?"

"It's just that we come from two different worlds, Macha!" Eastman said.

"You told Tashi once you might allow Wabakashiek to marry Eliza," Macha reminded him.

"I was joking," Eastman said. "But I do remember that. We were both concerned about how fast our children were growing up. Tashi told me, with Guy and Sam now gone, there were no boys or girls in your village left his age. I was sad that Eliza and John had no children their age to play with. Look, I'm really glad that John has made friends with your son Dyami. But Eliza is not even 18 years old yet. Even if I were comfortable with her marrying an Indian, which I am not, I do not want her to marry the first boy she meets. Therefore, Clara is right. It is best Eliza spends four years at boarding school. We will leave in a few days!"

"You cannot deny true love, no matter how old it is," Macha said. "You will break Wabakashiek's heart by doing this."

"Perhaps he will find someone more suitable for him while she is gone," Eastman said.

"Only if he also leaves you! Which he doesn't want to do!" Macha replied. "But, when he and Tashi are back, I shall tell them of your plan. If he agrees that you have betrayed him after everything he has done for you, you should not expect them to return to your farm. However, they are stubborn men. I will not tell them they cannot go to your farm as they will not listen."

Eastman waked as briskly as he could back to his farm.

"Eliza?" he called as soon as he walked through the front door of the house. "Please come down here. I need to speak with you! You too, Clara."

Yes, Papa?" she replied. Clara also came to his side.

"I understand you have taken quite a fancy to Mr. William Redskin. Sweetheart, that really isn't going to work out. The differences between his culture and ours are so significant, there really isn't any way you two could have lasting happiness. Therefore, your mother and I have decided it is best that you receive an appropriate education away from the farm. There is a school for young ladies in Benicia to which we will take you. We will leave on Monday to ensure you are there in time for a new school year."

It was a Saturday when Eastman broke this news to his daughter, who promptly broke down in tears. Not saying a word, she ran back up the stairs, with Clara following.

"I will try to help her to understand it's for the best, Ralph," Clara said. I am sure by Monday she will be excited about this new chapter in her life."

"I hope so, Clara," Eastman replied. "What I need to focus on, and what I also need William to focus on, is getting our 1,200 acres of cropland planted. I'm not going to be able to hire as much help from the village as I was planning, because I can subtract $300 out of my budget to pay Eliza's school tuition instead. That means I hire Tashi, maybe one or two other men to help with the planting. Not five or six. That's a lot of grain for four men to plant by themselves though. And I won't be there to oversee for more than a month!"

"Also, we'd better harvest up your garden, Clara," he continued. "We're going to need to stop in Stockton on our way to Benicia. We can sell some produce there. If you want to do some canning to sell, that would be good too. You know what to do! You made it through a year as a single mother back in 1851 and 1852. This time, we just need to stretch so we can spend $300 right quick."

"I'll get right onto the garden as soon as I get Eliza to understand," Clara said.

"William and Tashi are building some interesting contraption down by William's hut," Eastman said. "It's a raft long enough to span the entire river. I am not sure why. I am not even sure where they are. Macha says they left yesterday for Mariposa. "

"You will, then, talk to them about our intentions for Eliza?" Clara asked.

"They have no say in this matter, Clara," Eastman replied. "But yes, I will let them know. William would be worried about her if I did not. As for Tashi, the further I keep anyone in that village away from Eliza, the better off we all probably will be."

Wabakashiek and Tashi were already back to the wiki-up by the time Eastman arrived. They had started the process of driving their 6-inch nails through the outer beams and into the dirt on the south side of the river.

"William! Chief Tashi!" Eastman said. "Pull your raft over to my side! I need to talk to you about something."

"This raft will not go from side to side," Wabakashiek explained. It will stay in one place, one end on one bank, the other on the opposite bank. You can give us a hand. Grab a hammer!"

"May this please wait?" Eastman said. "What I need to tell you is very important."

"All right," Wabakashiek said, grabbing the smaller raft he and Tashi had taken to Mariposa. The two crossed over to Eastman by standing on their portable raft, then pushing the water with sticks until it reached the opposite bank some 30 seconds later. When they were on the north side, they approached Eastman.

"What is more important than getting that side of the river cleared?" Wabakashiek asked.

"I have decided, along with Mrs. Eastman, it is time for Eliza to leave the farm," Eastman began.

"What? Leave the farm! No, it cannot be time to leave the farm! We have to plant 1,200 acres this year!" Wabakashiek interrupted. It's going to take me several days just to get these last 400 acres plowed. And that's after we get this super-spanning raft built, so we can easily cross back and forth."

"Well, you and your father can work on that while we are gone," Eastman replied.

"You mean you are going to leave soon? With Eliza?" Wabakashiek could hardly control his feeling of rage as he questioned Eastman. Yet, a lack of discipline could make either Eastman or his father angry, so he found it best to keep his composure, regardless of how hard it would be.

"Yes, we cannot start the journey on the Lord's Day, so we will hold off until Monday. We will drop Eliza off at a school in Benicia, California. Benicia is near the San Francisco Bay, so it will probably take us a month to get there and back. Longer if the school hasn't started when we arrive."

"And then you will just leave Eliza there forever?" Wabakashiek asked.

"She will come home during summer for about eight weeks," Eastman said. "Then she will finish the school in four years. That is, if she does not meet and marry a suitable man before then, in which case she will take up a new residence in his home. That is what I'd like to see happen. If she returns to the farm after she graduates, there will be no opportunities here for her to have a decent life."

"She and I could have a decent life together!'" Wabakashiek said. "I love her, and I would care for her, even after you are long gone. And, while it is your people who have made life harder for our people, we have lived right here, on this river not two miles over that hill for as long as anyone can remember. If she was not happy living that way, why did you force her to do so all these years? Or is it me you are not happy with?"

"I am very happy with you, William," Eastman said. "But you and your people are built for this place. Us, we are only here because gold mining wasn't what I had hoped it would be. Perhaps when I figured that out I should have packed my whole family into a wagon and headed back to St. Louis. But it was a six-month journey over mountains way taller than those next to Sonora and Mariposa. We had to go over both of them getting to California when we came out. I did not want to go through that again. So I came down here. It has gone well for me, thanks to your help. I thought others would settle down here by the time Eliza and John grew up. But that has not happened. So now, I must give Eliza the experience of being with other people who are more like her. It is the only way she can have a meaningful life. We will leave Monday."

"As for today, if you can get this raft to span all the way across the river, wonderful. I also hope you will join us at the house tomorrow. After worship, we will have a special dinner, after which you can say good-bye to Eliza, since I don't know when, or even if, you will see her again."

"I will always love Eliza!" Wabakashiek said. "But if you do not view me as being as good enough for her, I am very sorry we ever met. It would be my hope that once you take Eliza away from me, you also go back to wherever it is you come from, and do not come back without her!"

"The property is mine" Eastman replied. "Even Shehamniu belongs to me. I let all of you live here out of the kindness of my heart and because you have been a big help to me. But my daughter is also mine, and I will do what is best for her."

Eliza had run out of the house when her mother tried to reason with her about the plan. She stood by Wabakashiek's wiki-up, out of the men's view, listening to most of their conversation. When she heard her father say he was doing what was best for her, she could no longer control her rage and ran down to the bridge.

"You are not doing what is best for me!" she screamed. "You are only doing what is best for yourself. Wabakashiek loves me, and will love the children we could have together. But if we create a family, he will have to provide for them. Now, he does everything for you, and all you do is treat him like someone whose feelings don't even matter! How would you feel if you had to plant all these fields yourself, because he and his whole village decide to no longer help you. That is what you would deserve!"

"You will not speak to me that way, Eliza!" Eastman said. "You will be leaving Monday for Young Women's Seminary. It is time you learned how to be a genteel lady, not this savage you are turning into. And I will not be a grandfather to Redskin children!"

"That is exactly what you will be a grandfather to, and a father to as well," Eliza said. "Because I am going to be Mrs. William Redskin, and my children's last name will also be Redskin."

"That is the most irrational thing I have ever heard, Eliza!" Eastman replied. "Now will you please go back to the house? I am going to take a switch to you if you don't, and you really are too big of a girl to switch. I would prefer your mother handle this insolent attitude of yours and when I come home for lunch, we will figure out how."

Eastman turned to Wabakashiek, but by that time he had left. He and his father were descending the hill to go back to Shehamniu. Eastman could see Wabakashiek angrily gesturing to both the raft and to him, but couldn't make out what the two were saying.

CHAPTER 12

"So you two are not going to work on that big project you had to go all the way to Mariposa to get nails for just yet?" Macha asked. "Why is that?"

"That man is lucky we don't have the fields planted," Wabakashiek said. "If they were, I'd burn them down. What I think we should do instead is, come Monday, we should get the raft and bring it over here. We can turn it back into lumber. Then let's steal his wheat seed and whatever animals he doesn't take with him on the trip he is going on, and we can use them to purchase good things in Mariposa. We don't need that fool."

"Eastman plans on taking Eliza away," Tashi explained. "Wabakashiek is furious, and quite frankly, so am I. The way he sees it, there are no suitable marriage partners for her in Shehamniu, so she will live somewhere else for four years. It is Eastman's hope she finds another man while she lives there. But, I am not sure she will. When she learned of this plan, I have never seen a girl talk so disrespectfully to her father. He threatened to whip her. If it had been my daughter, she would have been whipped right then, right there. But then, I would never tell my daughter the man she had grown up with for more than half her life, and has now come to love, was not good enough for her. Even if he were a White man. I've always known those White men cannot be trusted. I thought Eastman was an exception, but he sure proved he's just as evil, if not more so, than all the rest this afternoon. "

"Eastman and I had a conversation a few hours ago. He had just returned from Stockton. I'm not sure why he came down here, but I relayed the conversation we had yesterday. It was as you say, Tashi. I figured though, you two are too proud to not do the right thing."

"You are absolutely right we are proud," Tashi said. "They will be gone until the end of September. In the meantime, Wabashiek and I will do what is best for all of us. I am not sure stealing from Eastman is. It could bring law enforcement back down here from the mountains. They would kidnap some more children, and do who knows what to them.

"So, I think what we will do is take our big raft down here and attach it by our village, rather than his farm. It will make it easier for us to cross over the river, find the animals and the plants on the other side," Tashi continued. "Plus, if the White man figures out how to sail rafts, if we build two of these big ones on either side, he cannot come through the water to our village, our big rafts will block his way. Since we can hunt all the way up in the mountains, Wabakshiek is right. We do not need Eastman anymore. Even though food is more scarce than before he and the White men up there arrived, we can get by. Plus, we can still trade baskets with those White men. We don't need to steal Eastman's supplies. We can make it without his help whatsoever."

"I will have to organize a hunting party soon," Tashi added. "I can take Wabakashiek, Achachak, and some of the other men. In the meantime, Macha, you can lead the women to gather acorns. The trees are already ripe with them."

It took the Eastman family almost two weeks to go by covered wagon from their farm to Benicia. School started Monday, Sept. 2, which required the entire family to stay in the area an additional week, returning to their farm Friday, Sept. 13, 1861. It was still a little early to plant, but Eastman had thought William would return to his senses and to the farm. He thought he would see the additional 400 acres leveled.

Eastman was not prepared for what instead awaited him. Not only did the fields look exactly as he had left them, the animals looked skinnier. They had not been fed in five weeks. "William," Eastman called out heading down to the river. "What's going on with my animals? Why haven't you fed them? Why haven't you plowed the last 400 acres?"

Eastman then noticed. There was no bridge spanning on or across the river. And William's wiki-up was missing too. He headed over the hill to Shehamniu, hoping to understand why a whole village of men had been so neglectful of his property. There he saw the bridge attached to the two banks of the river, just as William and Chief Tashi had originally planned on his farm.

Tashi, Achachak and Wabakashiek were all near their wiki-ups, making arrowheads, when Eastman approached. The three completely ignored him. Macha and some of the other women were nearby, preparing loaves of both fry bread and acorn bread. They looked up, but said not a word when Macha put a finger to her lips.

Achachak and Macha's 12-year-old son, Dyami, broke the silence. Dyami had become good friends with John Eastman. Since no one had told him exactly what Eastman was up to, he still felt connected to the Eastman family. He ran to Ralph Eastman and hugged him.

"I am so glad you have returned, Mr. Eastman. "My mama and papa told me you were not coming back, that you and Mrs. Eastman, and John and Eliza were gone for good. I am glad they were wrong."

"Yes, Mrs. Eastman, and John are back at home," Eastman said. "They would be very happy to see you, Donald. Run on over there and say hello. I need to speak with William, Chief Tashi and your father."

"You have no further business with us!" Chief Tashi said. "Now go away!"

"I still have business with William," Eastman said. "Under the laws of Mariposa County, William is my son, and has been since 1851! He will be free to go his own way when he is 30 years old, and if what he told me is right, that's not until 1870. Nine years from now."

"He is an adult. Guyape and Sahale are younger than him, and they have been living on their own for several years now. He has chosen to make his life with us, and it is his hope that Eliza will be given an opportunity to make decisions for herself as well. We believe her love for Wabakashiek is so strong, she will choose him over you."

"I will not go back to the farm with you, Eastman," Wabakashiek said. "If you try to force me to do so, you'd better be good with a gun. We went to Mariposa while you were gone. I got me a gun while I was there and I am prepared to use it against you. I have that little respect for you because of what you have done. If you ever come back to Shehamniu, you had better have Eliza with you. Otherwise, I have no use for you."

Legally, Eastman could have gone to a Justice of the Peace and brought law enforcement to Shehamniu to get William Redskin back in his custody. He chose not to, which is probably a good thing. Without his knowledge, county lines in California shifted quite a bit during the first 11 years of the state's history.

Mariposa County, especially, had greatly shrunk in that time. In 1861, Eastman's farm was within the boundaries of Fresno County, which had been established in 1856. Had Eastman wanted to bring deputies to his farm, it would have taken him away from the farm for another three days, just to drag one stubborn young man there who would no longer willingly stay with him or work for him, and who might even try to kill him.

"I'll tell you what," Tashi said. "Give Wabakshiek, myself and Achachak new horses. Pay us each $50, and we all three will help you grade and plant your field, and when the time comes, we will harvest it. You will not pay us in wheat any more. You can pay the $50 in portions, but you will pay us some now, you will pay us additionally throughout the year, and you will pay us in full when your grain is ready for harvest. Next summer, we will spend money when we go to Mariposa! Not baskets!"

"I like that idea," Macha said. "Every year, our women make many more baskets than we need. You take those baskets and give them away in exchange for the things YOU want. What say do we have in it? We do all the work, and you get all the benefit. It's time YOU did some work!"

"Quiet woman, Achachak said. "We grow the wheat, and you bake and eat the bread. You feed it to YOUR children."

"They're YOUR children too," Macha said. "And what is baking? It's work. I would love to go on a trip with you. But no, I stay here and take care of YOUR children."

"Well, you are to be admired for taking care of 10 children, Macha," Eastman said. "But right now, instead of arguing, I really need Achachak to come with Chief Tashi and William back to my farm. I will agree to paying them money. And I hope they will buy you a nice dress and bonnet when they go to Mariposa again. But none of us are going to have wheat or money if we don't get the fields plowed!"

Chief Tashi and Achachak worked willingly for Eastman, happy they would be paid with real money instead of the grain seeds they had been paid in for the last three years. Wabakashiek stayed on the farm only because his alternative would be to leave the area all together, and be even further away from Eliza when she returned. Wabakashiek missed Eliza terribly.

The school Eliza began attending in 1861 has long had a role in educating California's young women. It was established in 1852 as the Young Women's Seminary, but was relocated to Oakland and renamed Mills College in 1871. It is still in Oakland today, and still teaches only women. Today, those women receive a liberal and highly technical education, and both bachelor's and graduate degrees in more than 40 different majors.

In 1861, when Eliza Eastman was a young woman, it was still on property adjacent to Benicia Presbyterian Church, where founder the Rev. Sylvester Woodbridge Jr. had established it. In those days, it taught all women the same thing – Christian education. Rev. Woodbridge, a devout Presbyterian, had established the college with the intent of schooling young women in the ways of genteel society, which he believed were the appropriate ways for anyone who had been blessed by God's favor. In the early years, most of its students were "city girls" from San Francisco and Sacramento.

Rev. Woodbridge had sold the college to the first principal, Mary Atkins, in 1857. She grew the school by riding her mule through mining camps all over northern California, informing the families with teen-age daughters about the opportunity they had in Benicia to learn how to be genteel women. Thus, by the time Eliza Eastman arrived, there were plenty of other "rough and ready" young women similar to her. But none quite as rough as Eliza.

Since Eliza only grew up around boys, three of whom were "savages," she did not always conduct herself as a lady. She was also affected by not having attended regular school ever, and having no memory of church attendance. Like a modern unruly kindergartener, she simply did not know how to act around large groups of people.

At Young Women's Seminary, she frequently interrupted Mary Atkins during the lessons. She also would argue with Atkins when receiving instruction from her about the gospel. Since she had not regularly attended church, and because her father had not disputed the ideas William, Guy and Sam had presented from their tribal religion, Eliza was not certain the Bible was the only religious truth. She absolutely couldn't accept the doctrine taught at Young Women's Seminary, that financial blessings were a sign of God's favor, and those who received them were the only ones who could be certain of salvation.

"Mrs. Atkins, if this is true, why did God make Indians?" she asked in class one day. "Indians lived for many years just on what God gave them. God provided them trees to make houses, food to eat, and skins to wear. They never needed money. Why would he send them to Hell when they never did anything to hurt anyone?"

"God works in mysterious ways," Mary Atkins replied. She wasn't really sure how to answer Eliza's question, although Eliza was far from the first girl to ask it. She had wondered the same about both Native Americans and Blacks when she was growing up, and she had encountered other curious girls before she moved to California. In her previous six years at the Young Women's Seminary, all her students had been a little more refined, or a lot more refined. So, she found Eliza's brashness kind of refreshing.

Mary Atkins had grown up in northeastern Ohio with eight sisters and one brother. By the time she moved to California at the age of 36, she had spent plenty more time with young women. She had been a public school student, a teacher, a college student, and a principal for girls at three other schools prior to the Young Women's Seminary. In fact, she had come to California in 1855, because it seemed even more exotic than her other idea, serving as a missionary in Siam.

One day, after a session of intense debate between Eliza and the other girls in the class, she wanted to know more about the girl's motivation. She had been told Eliza grew up on a farm, and had been home-schooled after first grade, and she had no sisters. She did not know the family had adopted three Indian boys, one of whom Eliza now was in love with. She asked Eliza to join her for tea.

"Eliza, you are a very rough girl," she began. "I know it has been difficult for you to adjust to life in a city, with lots of girls, and lots of rules you haven't had to follow before. I know I have spoken to you often before to reprimand behavior of which I did not approve. But, today, I want to let you know I do admire your sensitivity to others, especially to the plight of the Indian people. I am curious, how are you so knowledgeable about this?"

"I grew up with three Indian boys, whose names were William, Guy and Sam. Well, actually they have Indian names that sound kind of like that, but my father gave them Christian names. He also taught them to speak English and how to measure things and count money, the stuff men need to know to get by. And he taught me, my brother and them about the Bible. But they taught me lessons about how they think God works, and it's not always the same. So I'm not sure which is true.

"Guy and Sam moved away about three or four years ago," she continued. "But William is with my Papa farming to this day. I am not sure why we had nothing to do with them before that, but after Guy and Sam left, we made friends with all the people from their village. I find them all very charming. Especially William. I am in love with him, and as far as I am concerned, as soon as I am done here, I will go back to our farm and I will marry him. I do not see why that is a problem."

"I am not sure it is, Eliza," Mary Atkins replied. "I do know this. You are still very young. Your life experience is limited, and it is my vision all my students, you included, can see the world as much bigger than the community you grew up in. That is certainly true for you, because your community is merely your immediate family and the Indian village nearby. In a way, you are less naïve than some of these girls, who grew up in the rich parts of our big cities, without knowing anything about the other cultures around them. Perhaps you will return to your farm, and perhaps you will bring the gospel and a better life to the Indians you already have met. Perhaps you will even marry one of them, it is not unheard of. But only God knows what your future will be after you complete four years of education here."

Even though going from the farm to the city, and being the only girl to one in a school full of them was difficult, Eliza came to very much enjoy her first two years at Young Women's Seminary. She learned Bible history, and how to apply it to her own life. The seminary also gave the young women a more complete academic education than they had received before, delving into such topics as literature, science, United States history and current events.

In the exact same years Eliza attended the Young Women's Seminary, the American Civil War raged on the opposite side of the country. Eliza learned the history of slave-keeping, the designation of slave and free states, the Underground Railroad, and the process by which President Abraham Lincoln had come into office. The young women in Benicia not only learned about these facts, but engaged in lively debate about what should happen.

Mary Atkins, who had met freed slaves when she lived in Ohio, was sympathetic to the plights of Negroes. Eliza shared her sympathy and was happy when Lincoln issued the Emancipation Proclamation in 1863. She rationalized that if the Negroes were obtaining freedom back east, the Indians should have the same freedom in California.

Etiquette and social graces were also part of the curriculum at Young Women's Seminary. They learned and put into practice menu planning, party hosting and table manners. Mary Atkins often invited the women of Benicia to join the young women as guests at these parties, and at other times had her students put on tea parties for each other. She also enjoyed having tea with them one-on-one.

Eliza especially enjoyed the one-on-one teas she had with Miss Atkins. During these, they discussed literature and current events. Miss Atkins was the first person who had accepted without argument the opinions Eliza presented. Her parents and even William would often attempt to correct her thinking.

The Young Women's Seminary met from late August or early September to mid-June with two weeks off for Christmas, a week-long semester break in January, and one more week at Easter. The only way to return to the farm in the 1860s was by covered wagon, so Eliza had not planned to return to the farm until summer. It is unlikely the covered wagon roads were passable that first Christmas break anyhow, due to the Great Flood of 1861-62.

In this flood, the cities along the San Joaquin River and its tributaries sustained severe flood damage. So did Shehamniu and Eastman's farm. During previous floods, the Yokut and Miwok people who dwelt on the valley floor evacuated to higher ground and simply rebuilt their villages when they could. It usually wasn't long before life returned to normal.

But in December 1861 and January 1862, the flood was especially problematic. No one took an official total of rainfall that long ago, but it was enough rain to completely wipe out anything within three miles of the San Joaquin Valley rivers. Making things even worse, by 1861 those still in the mining industry were largely relying on hydraulic mining. In these operations, miners forced large amounts of water through devices that concentrated the flow, thereby dislodging large sections of the river bank. From the dislodged dirt, the miners found more gold than they had in years.

For those downstream, this was disastrous when it rained. The now-widened river banks allowed more rain to flow unimpeded down the rivers. Even without this practice, the rivers flooded their banks every year. With nothing upstream to hold it back, even more water came, causing even more water to flood over the banks when the river came to its flatter course. Thus, there most likely never was, nor ever will be a storm as devastating as the Great Flood of 1861-1862.

In Shehamniu, the adjustments required by this flood required many in the village to make permanent changes. They could not simply move up to the higher ground of their territory as they had before. For several years, they had been going into the other tribes' territory, and had either hunted there or bargained with the White business owners for food and supplies. It would be necessary to stay in the mountains until the flood receded.

Wabakashiek and Tashi went as a family with Achachak, Macha, Aloette, Dyami and the six youngest children in their large family. They had always operated as one family unit, ever since Wabakashiek's mother had passed away when he was 3 years old. Now Achachak and Macha's two oldest sons, Gosheven and Enyote, were already in Mariposa, so the family intended to stay with them. Since the oldest sons lived in a single wiki-up, it was necessary for the 12 newcomers to quickly build several additional ones, and to purchase blankets to cover the snowy ground beneath them.

Also traveling to Mariposa with this family of 12 were Ralph, Clara and John Eastman. The flood had completely wiped out Eastman's fall crop. In order to have enough money to pay for Eliza Eastman's schooling the following year, he needed to work for someone else as well. He found work at the same lumber mill where Gosheven and Enyote were employed. The Eastmans decided to rent a home from a Mariposa gold miner who had returned to the East Coast.

All of the visitors from Shehamniu, including the Eastmans, kept in touch with each other while they were in Mariposa. They came up to Mariposa in the middle of December. One of them, usually, Wabakashiek, served as a scout, going down to the base of the plateau that had served as the dividing line between the Chaushilha tribes and their mountain counterparts. It was late January when things were finally dry.

When the waters had receded enough to return, Eastman was eager to return home to replant the crops. He was paying the village men $25 more, so Tashi and Achachak shared his enthusiasm to return. Wabakashiek, on the other hand, still felt indifference about working for Eastman. What he missed was Shehamniu.

Even though Eastman needed a few others besides Tashi, Achachak and Wabakshiek to help him, not many from Shehamniu wanted to come back. In all, only about 25 people returned from Mariposa. For many years, Eastman continued to hire former Shehamniu residents during the planting and harvesting seasons. But other than Wabakashiek, Chief Tashi, and the family of Achachak, very few Chaushilhas resided in Shehamniu permanently after the flood of 1861-62.

Ralph and Clara Eastman returned the same time as the small group still planning to permanently reside in Shehamniu. Not returning with them was John Eastman. He had enrolled after Christmas break at Mariposa School. Although, in age, he was only as old as the sixth-graders who went to school with him, the education Clara Eastman had provided left him quite able to handle the eighth-grade curriculum. Since John enjoyed school, and had never had that opportunity to be with White children his age, the Eastmans decided he should stay with a family in Mariposa to finish out the school year.

Mariposa School awarded John a certificate of completion that spring. Since there was no high school in Mariposa in those days, Mariposa School also provided a program for students in grades 9 through 12. John Eastman, like his sister Eliza, came home during the summer of 1862. He then returned to Mariposa to live with the other family during the school year, and graduated from Mariposa School in 1866 at the age of 16. After graduation, he studied agriculture at the newly-formed University of California.

When Eliza returned home for summer in 1862, she was saddened to see the village of Shehamniu decimated to a mere 25 residents by the winter flood. Still, she was glad Wabakashiek was one of the few who had decided to stay close by. Wabakashiek and Eliza renewed their close friendship that summer. Wabakshiek told her about having to live in Mariposa with his cousin Gosheven for six weeks that winter. Eliza told him about Mary Atkins, and the many topics they had discussed.

"She truly believes all people are created by God as equals," Eliza said. "She has helped me to see clearly, anyone who exhibits bias against others merely because of the color of their skin is not understanding the Lord clearly." Eliza and Wabakashiek had similar conversations when she was home on summer break in 1863.

But Mary Atkins was in search of more adventure, and left the Young Women's Seminary. At the end of the 1862-63 school year, she sailed to Hawaii. She met Susan and Cyrus Mills, whom she would sell the school to in 1866. She then spent a year in Europe before returning to Ohio and teaching school for a few more years before finally getting married at the at the age of 50. Miss Atkins did return to Benicia in 1882 after her husband's death, but by then Eliza was a wife and mother of eight.

Once Miss Atkins left, the Rev. Woodbridge took over instruction, and Mrs. Linda Blake, a local widow from the Presbyterian Church, became the house mother. The Rev. Woodbridge was also sensitive to the abuses the Native Americans were enduring in post-Gold Rush California. But he was not as forward thinking as Mary Atkins had been, or if he was, he never shared those thoughts with Eliza beyond the teacher's desk and the pulpit. Although she may have learned more about the world around her in her final two years of seminary, Eliza didn't think it was relevant. She knew her future was with William Redskin, and the people of Shehamniu. She longed for the day she could return for good.

CHAPTER 13

Eliza Eastman graduated from Young Women's Seminary on June 16, 1865, and returned with her parents to their farm on July 1. She was much more aware of the world around her and how she should apply her Christian faith to the situations in which she found herself. She also knew she would not go very far from the farm when she returned. Her plan, which she told no one about until they were almost back to the farm, was to move to Shehamniu as William Redskin's wife.

"Papa, as you know, one thing I learned about in school was that in other states some people kept Negros as slaves," she said to Eastman as they approached the area Eliza had become familiar with as a child. "I learned, two years ago, Congress passed a law abolishing Negro slavery. I think there should also be a law against Indian slavery. That's what William is to us, a slave. It ought to be against the law!"

"William is not, nor was he ever a slave," Eastman replied. "I legally obtained custody of him before I moved you, your mother and brother down from Sonora all those years ago. I legally could have kept him in my custody until he was 30, which would have been five more years still. But, as you know he has been very angry with me for the last four years. He has returned to Shehamniu. I pay him, his father and his uncle very good wages now!"

"Well, I hope you will keep William very happy," Eliza said. "Because if he decides he does not want to work on the farm anymore, he will go somewhere else. And I will go with him, because I am going to be Mrs. William Redskin!"

"I don't know about that!" Eastman replied. "William hardly ever even mentions you anymore. All he does is work. And how would a girl with a college education live in an Indian village with a bunch of savages?"

"If we live in a hut, it will be fine with me. I have learned how to make any place in which I live a home, and that is what I will do!" Eliza replied.

"Eliza, that is ridiculous," Clara said. "You have lived in comfortable homes all your life. You now have an education that would allow you to become a teacher or a nurse anywhere in California. We are only taking you back to the farm until you figure out what is your next option."

"But all of those options mean leaving you, and Papa!" Eliza replied. "I don't want to do that. And I definitely do not want to live without William! I am sure he feels the same way!"

When they arrived at the farm, Eliza kept her word about Shehamniu. She immediately ran over the hill between her farm and the village, as fast as a young woman can run in a long skirt, bloomers and hob-nailed boots. The late afternoon sun was setting behind her when she arrived at Shehamniu, and Wabakashiek recognized her from her shadow. He was playing Spear and Hoops with some of the young children in the village. He immediately dropped his spear and ran to her.

"Eliza! You have returned!" he said. Without concern for what the children would think, since the people of Shehamniu had never had such concern, he grabbed her and kissed her for about a minute.

"Yes William, I am back," she replied when they came up for air. "Now, shall I help these children roll the hoops, or would you like me to help Macha get some acorn mush ready?"

"Those are not things for a White woman," Wabakashiek said. "Especially not one who has just graduated from college. I shall ask Macha to make something very special for you, and she will, even if I have to hunt it myself!"

"What, you are going to get your deer by nightfall, and then you want me to season and cook it for dinner tonight?" asked Macha. The children watching Wabakashiek kiss Eliza had giggled loudly, and she came to see what was causing commotion. Though pleased to see Eliza back in the village of Shehamniu, she was not pleased that Wabakshiek would expect her to whip up a special meal on short notice.

"Good afternoon, Macha. I shall be very pleased to help you prepare whatever food you have available," Eliza said.

"I am making some fry bread," Macha said. "I have squash and peppers in the garden, we can roast those too. And when Wabakashiek went up to the store in Mariposa a few days ago, he bought these wonderful brown beans, as well as a special pot for cooking them. Much easier than baskets! I happen to have them on the fire. So, it may not be a fatted calf or venison, but it's a good meal."

"May I help you roast the vegetables then, Macha?" Eliza asked. "I may as well be helpful if I am going to become part of your village!"

"Why would you become part of Shehamniu?" Macha asked. "Didn't you like living in a big city the last four years? Haven't you slept in a comfortable bed with a mattress all your life? How would you adjust to our ways? And where?"

"What I have learned in seminary is that all people are loved by God, regardless of the color of their skin," Eliza said. "In other parts of our country, the United States of America, there are people with very dark skin, much darker than any of you have. You could even say their skin is black, well certainly you can if your people have red skin. They are called Negroes. Their ancestors were brought from a place called Africa a century or more before this, and all of them were kept as slaves by farmers in other states besides California. California was supposed to have been a "free" state, so farmers here were not allowed to have Negro slaves. So what do they have instead? Indian slaves!

"Well, the man who was president of the United States for most of my time in seminary was Abraham Lincoln. He freed the Negro slaves," Eliza continued. "What I do not understand is why he did not also free the Indian slaves. Your people were here before us! We should not be taking you prisoner. What my father did to William, Guy and Sam was wrong. I am glad my father did not try to force him to return to live in the hut away from the rest of you. But I love William, and I want to be with his people!"

"I love Eliza too," Wabakashiek said. "But Eliza, there is a custom we have not followed for many years but certainly could in your case. Back when there were many Indian villages, the men in ours usually went to live with the women in other villages. They would fall in love, and they would not come back home until one year after the marriage ceremony. Then our men would come to our village, and the husbands of our women would return to their villages.

"Of course, lately, there have not been too many women from other villages for our men to meet, since the Whites have taken most of the people from the mountain villages as their prisoners, and disease has killed many people from the villages to the west of us. I bet I would not be the first man from my village who has fallen in love with a White woman, but I don't know since even Guyape and Sahale have left and never come back.

"So, what I would like to do is go back to your farm, and live with you. I would even be willing to build you a nice house if your father will help me. If that happens, since your houses are very strong, and since our village is very close by, we would not come back. But since you want to be part of my village, and my family, you will be. We will visit them often, and our children will know their grandfather, Chief Tashi."

"What we must do first is provide an offering to your parents," Tashi said. "We shall give them back the three horses they gave us when Eliza went off to college. We shall also give them one cow. And we will invite them to come here for a venison dinner two weeks from now. At this dinner, we will unite Wabakashiek and Eliza in marriage. Eliza, you will need to return to your parents' home until that time. Would you like to join us for dinner, and then Wabakashiek and I will walk back with you to discuss your engagement?

"That would be splendid," Eliza replied. "Macha, I will help you prepare."

It was still somewhat light, around 8 p.m., when they finished their dinner and went back to the Eastman farm. Ralph and Clara Eastman both saw their daughter, and went out of the farm house to greet the trio. Since they were returning the horses, each was riding one of them.

"Eliza, where have you been since we got home?" Eastman asked. "Your mother had no help preparing dinner, and now yours is cold. Did we spend $300 a year for the last four years for you to learn such terrible manners?"

"I am sorry Papa, but it was necessary to see Wabakashiek again. And yes, I learned a lot about how to treat others with kindness and decency at Young Women Seminary. I am appalled that my own father took three young men as slaves –

"They weren't slaves!" Eastman interrupted. "They were boys I had custody of!"

"You took them into custody against the will of their families," Eliza said. "You drove two of them from their village permanently. But you won't do that to William. He has agreed to come and live on our farm again, as my husband. Traditionally, women who marry into Shehamniu move there with their husbands after one year of marriage, but William says, if you and men of his village will help, he will build a strong house for the two of us to live. And then, because it is a strong house, we will not leave the farm. We will stay on the farm, but we will visit Shehamniu anytime we wish!"

"So, William, you have asked for my daughter's hand in marriage? And you don't care what I think about it?" Eastman asked.

"I do want your blessing, and so does my father," Wabakashiek said. "That is why we are returning to you the horses you gave us after Eliza left for college. We also will give you one cow. I know, as many cows as you have, one more is a small gesture. However, it is a token of how much I want to have Eliza as part of my family. Will you please give your blessing, and will you, Mrs. Eastman and John please join our village in a banquet to unite and celebrate my marriage to Eliza?"

"If Eliza wishes, I will allow this," Eastman replied. "She did not meet someone more suitable while she was in Benicia, and as determined as she is to only love you, I doubt forcing her to go somewhere else will be of any benefit. And you really are a good man, William.

"I also appreciate that Eliza would like to have a banquet in Indian tradition, given that her last name will become Redskin," Eastman continued. "But, before this banquet, it will be necessary for her to be married, legally, in a church. My brother, Richard, is the senior warden of St. John the Evangelist Episcopal Church in Stockton. The two of you shall be married there, and he will perform the ceremony."

During the years Eastman had taken Wabakashiek, Guyape or Sahale to Stockton with the grain harvest, they had always visited St. John the Evangelist Episcopal Church there. Eastman had wanted the boys to experience true church. Had he lived close enough to a church to attend regularly during any of his time in California he would have, as he believed church to be a key to a civilized society.

"What I propose to do is take all of you, and also Achachak and his family, to my brother's church in Stockton when these fields are harvested. I'll have to go up there and get a second covered wagon first, so William, you can come with me to help with that. I'm going to have to go up to Mariposa first and get John, and I'll bring him to Stockton with us as well. We will secure the church for later this summer. Eliza, you and Clara can stay home and figure out all the women things, like wedding dresses and flowers and what not."

"Thank you Papa, for agreeing to let me marry William," Eliza said.

"Mr. Eastman, I assure you I will work hard and take very good care of Eliza," Wabakashiek said. "I will even accept your name for me, William Redskin, if that will help me to be a better husband. I will do everything I can to provide for her the best life she could ever have. Thank you for blessing our upcoming marriage."

CHAPTER 14

The preparation for William and Eliza's wedding began immediately. Since John was still in Mariposa, Ralph Eastman left the next morning, with Eliza and Clara, to fetch him from the family he stayed with during the school year. This also gave the women an opportunity to shop for what they needed for the upcoming nuptials.

In 1865, women traditionally did not opt for fancy gowns they would never wear again. Instead, wedding dresses became their Sunday best. The fabric shops in California reflected that trend, so the best material Clara and Eliza could find was an off-white linen. They chose a pattern with a four-tier skirt with crinoline, a tight bodice and a high neckline. To each tier, and to the neckline of the dress, they attached bobbin lace. Clara had learned how to make this type of lace as a girl, so the lace adorning -Eliza's dress was homemade. Two other items purchased in Mariposa for Eliza were flat white satin shoes and a garnet pendant, as this was Eliza's birthstone. Since she would become Eliza Redskin, they also purchased a solid-color deep red fabric from which they made a maid-of-honor dress for William's cousin Aloette, who would serve as Eliza's maid of honor.

Clara and Eliza also took it upon themselves to make dresses for Clara, Macha and all of her daughters, and suits for the men and boys. Since this was California, where dust was a way of life, even a wedding suit came in black. Each man wore the suits with pressed white cotton shirts. William wore a tie made from the same linen as the bride's dress, and the rest of the men red ties from the fabric of Aloette's dress.

Clara had made dark blue cotton dresses for her, Macha and Macha's daughters. This included a second dress for Aloette. This was the same type of dress Clara and Eliza wore every day. Macha and her daughters typically only wore deerskin skirts and cloth shawls, but Clara had hoped they would also enjoy wearing this more modest dress after the wedding.

Eliza had collected the addresses of some of the other young women in the Class of 1865 at the Young Women's Seminary. She had purchased fine paper, envelopes and a fountain pen in Mariposa. Since she had learned calligraphy at the school, she was able to write in elegant script "Mr. and Mrs. Ralph L. Eastman request the honor of your presence at the wedding of their daughter, Eliza Frances Eastman, to Mr. William Redskin on Saturday, Aug. 19 at 2 p.m. at St. John the Evangelist Episcopal Church, 316 El Dorado St., Stockton, California."

She addressed each invitation in an equally elegant script, finishing all of them before her father, fiancé and brother left for Stockton. This would allow her fellow students, who all could receive mail either at their homes or at a nearby post office, to be notified of her upcoming nuptials and possibly attend.

After an overnight trip to Mariposa, the Eastmans celebrated the Fourth of July with the people of Shehamniu, who at that point had come to accept their village as part of California and the United States. The next morning, Eastman, his son John, and Wabakashiek left by horseback for Stockton. There they met with Richard Eastman, who introduced them to the church priest, the Rev. Elijah Birdsell. Among the original 10 members of the church congregation, there had been a Native American boy, probably about the same age as Wabakashiek. Remembering this, Richard Eastman was completely accepting of his niece's plans for matrimony and graciously welcomed Wabakashiek into the family.

They secured St. John the Evangelist Episcopalian Church for the wedding on Aug. 19, 1865. They also obtained a marriage license at the San Joaquin County Courthouse. It was here that Wabakashiek officially became William Louis Redskin. Had he insisted on keeping the name Wabakashiek it is unlikely the court officials would have issued the license, but with a "White" sounding first and last name, he was able to obtain it without questioning.

Since they would be taking 16 people to Stockton for the actual wedding, it was necessary to obtain a second covered wagon while they were in Stockton. The wagon in which Eastman had brought his family to the farm back in 1852 could not comfortably hold more than eight. They also purchased eight additional oxen.

The logistics of getting three horses, three men, eight oxen and one covered wagon from Stockton back to the farm required two men, William Redskin and John Eastman, to ride two of the horses, with the third horse tied to William's mare. Ralph Eastman rode on the front of the wagon, guiding the oxen along the course of the San Joaquin and Chowchilla rivers. They returned to their farm on July 18, 1865 and immediately began the process of harvesting grain.

Since Eastman had 1,200 acres to harvest, it was necessary for him to hire additional men to help with the process of running his combines and threshers. He picked up Achachak and Macha's oldest sons in Mariposa. He also hired three other Chaushilha men there. Meanwhile, John, William, Tashi and Achachak began the process of harvesting the wheat.

The travel to and from Mariposa took Eastman eight days. With 12 men working from early morning to just before sundown, they harvested all 1,200 acres in 10 additional days. Then, they loaded it onto the trailer.

The three men from Mariposa built a raft for their journey back upstream. Everyone else left for Stockton. It was Aug. 5, 1865. They had exactly two weeks to get there in time for their church reservation. As was standard practice, they made it in 10 days, arriving in Stockton on Aug. 15. As had been the case since 1859, they made one stop at Henry Miller's trade post near the present-day city of Los Banos, where they sold him a portion of the grain.

William Redskin took the reins of the two horses pulling the grain trailer. Eastman himself took the wagon with Clara, Eliza, Macha, Aloette and four younger Shehamniu children. John, Chief Tashi and Abakachak took turns driving the rear wagon and otherwise riding along on the grain trailer or the front wagon. Dyami and his older brothers were almost always riding "shotgun" on one or the other wagon, and the other children stayed in the rear of the second wagon.

William Redskin and Eastman had by this time been to Stockton more times than they could remember. It had grown from a small village of less than 2,000 to nearly 7,000 people in those 13 years. This was far larger and grander than anything the rest of the people of Shehamniu had seen, as their trip to Mariposa was the farthest from home Macha, her daughters and several of her sons had ever taken from home, and quite different from the mountains above Mariposa where the men and older boys had hunted. Although the populations of Sonora and Mariposa were also relatively large during the Gold Rush and the years following, they never had the "big city" feel that Stockton had developed, so Clara, Eliza and John were also impressed with the size and grandeur of Stockton.

In 1865, Stockton already contained nearly 300 blocks. Although the streets were not paved in 1865, they were neatly graded into near perfect squares, except on the waterfronts of the three rivers that converge in the city limits before emptying themselves into the San Francisco Bay. There, wooden sidewalks extended clear to the water, giving pedestrians easy access to stores, restaurants, saloons, hotels and other businesses. In the water, boats cruised to and from the bay, some of them clipper ships more than 200 feet long with sails extending more than 200 feet high.

"Whoa," Dyami said. "This is all amazing. Who would have thought anything like this existed in the same world we live in?"

"The world is becoming a much different place now," William Redskin said. "All of our lives have been changing for nearly 20 years now. I bet when you grow up Dyami, they will change even more. And by the time we have grandchildren, we will not recognize this place as where we grew up at all."

"It certainly is a different world here already," Macha said. "I have to call you William now, when I have called you Wabakashiek all your life. And we have headed to this strange place called Stockton so you can take Eliza as your bride, when everyone who was married before you simply was blessed by our tribal chief before leaving their parents' home to establish their own. This is very different. But there is one thing I hope will not change. I would like to see grandchildren, and I would like to see them before our world in what was Shehamniu completely changes into something more like this."

"I agree!" Clara said. "I do remember St. Louis, Missouri, where Ralph and I grew up, looking like this. I have missed the life a big city like this has to offer. But Eliza, don't you dare run off to here, or to Benicia, or San Francisco or anywhere else like that. I too want to enjoy my grandchildren!"

"I would not think of it!" William Redskin said. "I have come to appreciate the things Stockton has to offer myself. But cities are not an easy place for Indians to live, so I would feel much safer making my home as close to Shehamniu and the Eastman family as possible. I would rather help Eastman with his farm any day than get a job in a city!"

"I love it on the farm too," Eliza said. "I never even cared for Benicia that much, and this city is even larger. Give me a home on the farm any day."

The St. James the Evangelist Episcopalian Church was built in 1850 on El Dorado Street, one block from the southernmost river channel. It still stands to this day, and was just as grand looking in 1865 as it is now. It is a two-story brick building with stained glass windows and a tall steeple. Inside, a pipe organ extended almost to the top of the second story, which is open except for a choir loft in the sanctuary. In the adjacent part of the church was a fellowship hall and several Sunday school classrooms.

Richard Eastman and his family lived in a modest home, also on El Dorado Street. He had agreed to put up all 16 of the travelers there for the five nights they would be staying in Stockton. He had five children of his own, so that meant 23 people crammed themselves into the home. For Clara Eastman, it was a long-awaited reunion with her brother-in-law and his wife Caroline. For Eliza and John, it was the opportunity to meet cousins they either didn't remember, or in the case of Richard's three youngest children, had never met before. For the Native Americans traveling with them, including William, it was something completely new to take in.

Their first full day in Stockton, all of the men and boys tended to the business of selling the rest of the wheat. It was purchased by men who were in the business of shipping this wheat back around Cape Horn to the East Coast. In merely one hour's time, they had unloaded the trailer, received payment and were able to spend the rest of that day and most of the two following days fishing on the rivers.

Meanwhile, the women baked a wedding cake and assembled bouquets for Eliza and Aloette, who would serve as maid of honor. Eliza also created a floral head piece to attach to her veil. They also made corsages for Clara and Macha, and boutonnières for William Redskin, Ralph and John Eastman and Tashi. For Macha's youngest daughter, 4-year old Haiwee, they made a basket of flowers for her to carry as the flower girl. All the floral pieces were red roses accented with baby's breath. Since they also had to cut the flowers from Caroline's and other Stockton women's gardens, this took them two days. On the morning of the third day they went over to the Episcopal Church, where they tied silk ribbons to the pews and set up garlands of flowers on the alter.

Neither William nor Eliza had ever so much as seen a wedding before. Nor had anyone else in their wedding party. With this in mind, the Rev. Birdsell led them in a wedding rehearsal the afternoon before their wedding. The group then returned to the Eastman home and had a light dinner of soup and oyster crackers before getting ready for the important day to come.

The morning of the wedding, all 23 occupants of the house needed to take baths. For most of them, a dip in the Calaveras River sufficed. But for Eliza, Clara, Catherine, Aloette and Haiwee, real baths were necessary. They heated water on Caroline's stove and poured it into a large cast-iron tub, large enough for an adult to lay down in. Each woman and girl needed five pots of water, thus this pot was heated 25 times. Eliza also was to have her hair curled with a 19th century curling iron. These were, of course, not the electric devices of modern times. Instead, a woman heated the curling iron on her kitchen stove. With pot-holders, she carefully crimped the scorching hot iron onto another woman's hair, then wrapped the hair onto the iron, just as women do with electric curling irons today. Care had to be taken. If the curling iron was too hot, it could burn a woman's hair. There also was greater risk of burning a woman on the neck than with the modern curling irons. But, Eliza's Aunt Caroline successfully curled Eliza's hair into long, wavy locks. She then pinned the headpiece to both the veil and to Eliza's hair.

"You look absolutely beautiful, Eliza," she said. "I hope William can keep his hands off of you until tonight."

"Aunt Caroline, William is a perfect gentleman!" Eliza said. She knew, from a few previous encounters, it would not matter to William what she wore during the day. Once they were alone, and legally wed, he would not resist any further, nor would she deny him.

At the church, the men dressed themselves in their suits and awaited the arrival of the women. After they got themselves ready at the Richard Eastman home, the women and girls walked the four blocks down to the church. When they arrived at 1:45 p.m., Clara notified the Rev. Birdsell they were ready to begin.

The ceremony got underway at the scheduled time of 2 p.m. The Rev. Birdsell, best man John Eastman, and William Redskin waited at the front of the church. The guests seated already were the bride's uncle, aunt and five cousins, the groom's uncle and aunt, seven of his cousins, 12 people from St. John the Evangelist Church and five young women from Young Women's Seminary.

St. John's the Evangelist Episcopal Church already had a magnificent organ, played by Mrs. Abagail Nichols. She played the Eastman family's favorite song "Crown Him With Many Crowns" as Dyami escorted first Tashi, then Clara Eastman into the sanctuary. Maid of honor Aloette also made her way down the aisle during this song, escorting her little sister and flower girl, Haiwee.

Mrs. Nichols then began playing "The Wedding March," signifying for everyone to rise and watch as Ralph Eastman escorted his daughter Eliza to the front of the sanctuary. Eliza beamed as happily as any bride ever did. William watched, and having been well trained not to show emotion, simply closed his eyes and took in a deep breath.

"Friends, we have gathered today to witness the union of Eliza Frances Eastman to William Louis Redskin," the Rev. Birdsell began. "This is a couple who grew up together on what is truly frontier land, in the valley on a tributary of one of our great rivers. God strategically brought them together in this land, where they have come to love one another, and where they are called to live life together. This wedding will celebrate the beginning of a more complete togetherness as man and wife."

The Rev. Birdsell then read 1 Corinthians 13, which is the Love Chapter of the Bible. After another scripture reading, Genesis 3, by Caroline Eastman, the Rev. Birdsell led them through the vows:

"I William, take thee Eliza, as my lawfully wedded wife. I promise to love, cherish and provide for you all of my days, until we are parted by death."

"I Eliza, take thee William, as my lawfully wedded husband. I promise to love, honor and obey you for all of my days, until we are parted by death."

There was no exchange of rings, as this was uncommon for 19th century pioneers. After the vows, the church sang "My Faith Looks Up To Thee" accompanied by Mrs. Nichols on the organ.

The Rev. Birdsell then informed William "You may kiss your bride." After William and Eliza exchanged a short, sweet, lips-only kiss, he announced "May I introduce, for the first time, Mr. and Mrs. William Redskin!" Mrs. Nichols then played Mendehlson's Wedding March as the bridal party and wedding guests followed the couple out of the sanctuary.

After the ceremony, these guests celebrated the first reception with a buffet of ham, biscuits, jelly and fresh fruit, and wine for the adults, apple cider for the children. This had been prepared by other women from St. John the Evangelist Episcopal Church. William and Eliza then cut the cake the Eastman women had prepared, and served it to their guests.

After the wedding, William and Eliza walked to the Stockton Inn. The men, during the earlier trip to Stockton, had arranged for the couple to stay there on their wedding night. After they carefully hung their wedding clothes in a hotel closet, folded the inner garments and lined their shoes together, they looked at their naked bodies. It was William's first time seeing Eliza naked, and his desire immediately overtook him. They made love. When it was over, he cried out "Eliza, I love you. I thank my God and your God for you. I will love you forever."

The next morning, they dressed in clean regular clothes and walked back to Richard Eastman's home, as that very day they would begin the long trip back to the Ralph Eastman farm with the other 14 people who were returning to either the farm or Shehamniu. They returned on Aug. 30, 1865.

The next day, Tashi, Achachak, Macha and their family began preparation of a second wedding feast following Chaushilha tradition. Tashi, Achachak and three of Achachak's sons rode by raft to the mountains. Two of these were his oldest sons, who had come down for the wedding. They were returning to work responsibilities in Mariposa.

Before even reaching Mariposa, Tashi, Achachak and Dyami found and slaughtered a buck deer and returned it to Shehamniu the same day. It was the first deer Dyami had killed. However, his father and uncle didn't think it would be fair to deny Dyami part of the wedding feast. They decided, also, a young Native American boy in 1865 had already learned quite a bit about sharing what he had with others, and therefore wouldn't get the same benefit boys traditionally had received when denied their first deer.

Upon the men's return to Shehamniu, Macha and Aloette seasoned the deer and roasted it for two days on a fire. On that second day, they also boiled the pot of beans and roasted the squash and tomatoes that were left in their garden after a month of not being tended. They served this with Indian fry bread they also had just made.

They sent Dyami to summon William and Eliza, Ralph, Clara and John to join them in this meal. The guests enjoyed it so much, for the rest of Macha's life they gathered in what was left of Shehamniu annually the first weekend in September for a similar feast. Once Macha died, Eliza Redskin continued the tradition for the rest of her life, extending the invitation to the growing number of people who by then had moved into the community of what became Chowchilla.

In 1912, there were a growing number of White people moving to farms near the area where the Eastman and Redskin families were already farming. One of these newcomers, O.A. Robertson, purchased 134,000 acres and established a "city" with a sewer, buildings a rail spur and streets, including the stately palm-tree lined Robertson Boulevard that still serves as the city's main street to this day. It was Robertson who named the new city Chowchilla, honoring but corrupting the spelling of the Chaushilha tribe that had lived in the area before him. Robertson built his United States Farm Land Company Office, then held a rodeo and barbecue to begin selling off both farm and city lots within his vast holdings.

It's not clear if the informal gatherings people like Eliza Eastman held, or the city-wide beef barbecue O.A Robertson held in 1912 were the forerunners of the Spring Festival residents of Chowchilla have enjoyed for many decades now. What we do know is, regardless of race, color or ethnicity, most people in Chowchilla enjoy the Spring Festival and the Madera County Fair now held in conjunction with it. They also enjoy the coronation of a boy as Tommy Hawk, a girl as Little Miss Madera County and a young woman as Miss Madera County.

From its opening in 1916 and even now, more than 100 years later, the people of Chowchilla have also enjoyed rituals surrounding Chowchilla High School. For its first century, those rituals centered around the school's mascot "The Redskins."

Many Chowchilla residents by 2016 had at least a small portion of Native American blood. Some had it because their ancestors grew up as Chaushilha or other nearby tribes. Many more had this ethnicity from far away tribes, even Mexican-American tribes. But at some point, all these partially Native Americans or their ancestors moved to Chowchilla. They almost all were proud of their Native American heritage, and how Chowchilla celebrated it with Redskin Pride.

Unfortunately, the California State Legislature, oblivious to the contributions the Chaushilha made to Chowchilla's history, gave the school a most unwanted 100th birthday present in 2015. This was legislation prohibiting the use of Redskins as a mascot, which took effect at the end of 2016. The school then changed its mascot to "The Tribe." This is perhaps even more fitting, because it honors all Native Americans from what is now known as the Chowchilla Tribe.

Made in the USA
Middletown, DE
10 July 2021